A HOOD LOVE LIKE NO OTHER 2

OTHER 2

THE FINALE

NIKKI BROWN

SUPREME WORKS PUBLICATIONS

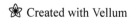 Created with Vellum

CHAPTER 1

$\mathcal{M}$ ira

Where we left off...

When I got back to the waiting area, Miracle was still there, and that pissed me off. My mom was keeping me sane while she was here, but she had to leave to get my kids, so it was just me, her, La, and my feelings about this whole situation.

I walked over and took a seat right in front of her. I needed her to give me the answers that Lake couldn't right now. I needed to know why she thought this was his baby. I had every intention on being civil with this hoe, but the way she looked at me threw all of that out the window.

"Why the fuck are you here?" I yelled at her, and she glared back at me like I was the one that was in the wrong. Her demeanor was confident, like she knew that she was the one that

was meant to be by his side through all of this. *"You heard what the fuck I said?"*

"I deserve to be here just as much as you do." Her tone was calm, but there was power behind her words, and I was eager to know where it came from, so I challenged her.

"Bitch, you're nothing but a side bitch. You do know that, right? He used you when we weren't getting along." I gave her a dose of reality. I didn't know what Lake told this girl to make her feel the way she felt, but she stood strong in her truth; too bad it wasn't real. *"What, he fucked you a couple of times and you lucked up and got knocked up with a baby that he doesn't even want or believe is his?"*

My words bothered her, I could tell. Her eyes twitched when I said it, but she was not about to let me know that, so instead of flipping, she calmly crossed her legs and swept the long strand of hair that fell out of the messy bun that was on top of her head.

"Oh, is that what he told you?"

"It ain't like that, baby. You know that baby ain't mine. I would never do no shit like that to you." I tried my best to mimic Lake. It was an epic fail, but she caught my drift.

"He and I both know that ain't true, and in the back of your mind, so do you. I think he was just trying to spare your feelings like I'm trying to do." Sitting back in her chair, she crossed her arms and glowered at me like she knew something I didn't.

"So, you're one of them, huh?" I scoffed. *"One of the delusional ones that make up whole relationships in your mind off a sample of the dick?"* I chuckled, but I didn't believe the words that came out of my mouth any more than she did. This girl was

2

too comfortable for her to just be a fling. I had a feeling she was about to tell me just how close she was with my man.

"That's just the thing; I didn't sample the dick. It's mine and has been for the last two years. Lake is more mine than he ever was yours." She smirked.

I did exactly what I said I wasn't going to do, I lost it. I stood up and punched her right in the mouth. She countered and hit me back with a two piece. She was quick with her hands, I would give her that because I never even saw it coming. We were going blow for blow until I felt myself being pushed back. I thought I was getting jumped, but then I heard Lala's voice, and I stopped.

"Y'all two chill the fuck out! Lake in that fucking hospital bed fighting for his life, and Heart is sitting in somebody's fucking jail right now, and y'all doing this?" The tears that cascaded down her face broke my heart, but I was too angry to show her any sympathy. I just wanted her to move out of my way so that I could get my hands on this bitch. "Both of y'all should be ashamed of yourselves!"

We both just stood there like raging bulls, ready to attack. Neither of us addressed what Lala had just said; we were just that pissed off. I loved La, but she didn't know what the fuck I was feeling at this moment. She wasn't going through what I was going through, so she didn't have the right to tell me to calm down.

"I don't even know why the fuck you're here," Miracle said to me. "I know if my man's side piece put me in the hospital, I wouldn't be."

Her words stung, but I would never give her the satisfaction *of seeing me sweat. She was right about one thing; I didn't know why I was here. Even though shit between me and Lake are fucked up, I couldn't imagine myself not being here for him at a time like this.*

"I didn't know side bitches had an opinion."

"I'm far from a side bitch, bitch!"

"Are y'all fucking serious?" La screamed to the top of her lungs. "Just stop! Lake lied to the both of you. If you gone be mad at anybody, be mad at him! You can't do that though, cause he is laying in there, and we don't even know if he gone make it, and y'all worried about who he fucked more?" Her eyes darted back and forth between me and Miracle. "Got damn!"

Before I could tell her how I felt about the situation, the door to the back opened, and Dr. Smire walked out. I turned my attention to him, praying that he was about to tell us something good, but the way he was looking told me otherwise.

"Dr. Smire." I stepped forward and waited for him to speak.

"It's touch and go right now. He's still on the ventilator, but like I explained before, there is brain activity. I need to know if things go south, who will be making the decision whether or not to keep him on life support?"

"What do you mean if things go south?" Miracle stepped up. "You have to save him!" she cried.

"I will be making the decisions." I rolled my eyes in her direction and focused my attention on the doctor. "I'm his fiancée and the mother of his kids; he doesn't have any family. He grew up in the foster system."

"No, she won't be making any decisions." Miracle started

fumbling around in her bag. "*I will.*" *She pulled out a piece of paper.*

"*No! What she is about to do is get the hell on away from here! She's not wanted! If Lake was woke, he would tell you that she is no one to him!*" *I yelled in her direction. I was tired of this girl, and she just kept coming like it was her duty.*

"*What's your name and your relationship to the patient?*" *Dr. Smire asked, completely ignoring my outburst. Miracle handed him the folded-up piece of paper. Lala and I looked at each other and then back at her.*

"*My name is Miracle Childs and I'm his wife!*"

iracle

"What the fuck did you just say?" Mira snatched my marriage license out of the doctors hands and examined the document. "She's fucking lying, this is not real." She said just above a whisper and for a second, I really felt sorry about all of this but she just wouldn't stop. The energy that she had before was gone, all the fight that she had just moments ago vanished.

"Miracle no." Lala looked at me with eyes full of tears but her feelings weren't on the top of my list of priorities because the way I looked at it she should have been consoling me right now instead of staring at me with judgmental eyes. "When? How?"

I watched as she tried to figure out how she missed the relationship between me and Lake. I wasn't about to help her understand, it wasn't her business, it was no one's business but mine and Lake's.

Turning to face the doctor he looked at me with sad eyes, it was bad enough that I had to deal with my husband laying in this hospital bed not knowing if he's gonna make it or not. Now I had to deal with this shit too.

"I'm sorry," the doctor started. "I just need to make sure that I know who to come to if things take another direction."

"I'll be here, I'm not leaving until his eyes are open." I nodded my head and he gave me a forced smile right before his eyes returned to the saddened state and he gave a look to Mira whose face was covered with tears.

The doctor gave me a few more details about everything that was going on and then he left behind the double doors that he came from. For a while no one said anything, I walked over and took the seat that I was originally sitting in.

I had no reason to explain myself to anyone, and I didn't plan on it. Mira hadn't moved from the spot that she was standing and you could see the pain etched all over her face but there was nothing that either of us could do about this situation but accept it and I hoped that she would for our children's sake.

"Miracle how could you do that? I told you that he was with Mira and they had kids. Why would you do something so low?"

"Lala this has nothing to do with you. I love you and you know that but please don't make this an issue." I didn't bother looking her way I just leaned my head back against the wall that was directly behind the chair that I was sitting in. Mira had yet to address the situation and I was glad because I was not trying to discuss this right now.

"Miracle you're my best friend and you lied to my face. You told me that you weren't fucking with Lake and here you are married. What the fuck?" she yelled and threw her hands on her hips.

"So how long yo little hoe ass been with my nigga?" Mira finally spoke up and I sat up in my seat just in case she ran up on me again.

I hated to fight while I was pregnant, but I wasn't about to let this bitch keep disrespecting me. Out of respect for Lake I was trying to be chill, she just kept pushing me. She started all of this shit, it's not my fault she didn't get the results that she wanted.

"We got married right before my 19th birthday." My birthday had just passed a few weeks ago, it was during the time that Lake thought it was okay to keep pulling disappearing acts on me.

"You think this shit cute huh?" she tried to rush me again but this time Lala jumped in front of her. "Move La, I'mma beat her married ass." She tried to get to me again but she was no match for Lala.

After trying her best to get through to no avail she balled up my marriage license and chucked it my way. I could see the hurt pouring from her eyes as she willed back the tears that were threatening to fall. I really didn't want her to find out like this but she left me no choice.

Lake and I talked about how we would tell her so many times, I just hated that he wasn't here for it. He's gonna be pissed because he stood a chance of losing his kids if she went on some vindictive shit. I was praying that wasn't the case but you never knew with some women. I just hoped the he understands that I had no choice.

"You know what? Fuck this shit. I hope his ass die in that fucking hospital bed!" she said through clenched teeth and I jumped to my feet.

"Mira!" Lala gasped and then put her hands on her hips. "I know this is a fucked-up situation and you hurt right now but don't say no shit like that. Lake is the father of your kids."

I tried to walk pass Lala to get to the bitch for coming out of her mouth like that but just like Lala held her back from getting to me, she held me back too. I stepped back and let the tears roll out of my eyes because there was a chance that he wouldn't come back to us.

"You don't know what I'm feeling right now Lala so don't tell me how to react. For the last almost seven years, I've been with this man, gave him two kids and this is what he does to me?" She pointed her finger in my direction. "I was there when this nigga ain't have shit. I was there giving him and Heart the money to reup when shit was rough. Where was this bitch, doing homework?"

"I ain't too young for Lake's heart." I yelled and she tried to slip past Lala. I was tired of the back and forth with her so I walked up and punched her in the eye and she swung over Lala's head and hit me.

"Got damn it stop before we all get thrown out." Lala tried her damnedest to separate us but we were too damned deter-mined to get to one another.

I ended up getting past Lala and me and Mira was going toe to toe. I had her in a corner and was wailing on her. She couldn't do nothing but cover her head and take the licks. I hated this shit had to come to this but no matter what the situation or how she looked at it, I wasn't about to be disrespected.

Lake never lied to me about her, he told me who she was and what she was in his life and that was just the mother of his kids. He loved me and I knew that so I dealt with the fact that he needed to be present in her life for the sake of the babies.

He never told her that he was married and that has nothing to do with me but what I won't do is deal with his bullshit. She finally hoovered in the corner that we were fighting in and I took a few steps back.

"Lake lied to you and I get it, but that's not my issue. Your issue is with him. Lake never lied to me about you and or your position in his life and because I *know* who I am to him and what we have I allowed him to handle things with you at his own pace. I know my place and I've played my position and none of that included being disrespected by you or anyone else." My voice tipped a few octaves as I struggled to catch my breath. "Now you have one of two choices, you can chill the fuck out and wait to see what the doctor says about Lake or I can have them throw you out. Your choice, but I will not keep going back and forth with you."

She looked up at me with a look that I couldn't decipher, slowly standing up she shook her head and walked passed me and then Lala. When she got to where her bag was she snatched it up and then turned to look at me with hate in her eyes.

"You know he told me just a few weeks ago that he was gonna marry me and spend the rest of his life making me happy." She said and scoffed. "I guess that will never be huh?" She shook her head and then looked me square in the eyes. "Y'all shit was built on a big ass lie. You know just like I do that shit will never last. I can't wait to see the same look in your eyes that's in mine right now." She turned her attention to Lala. "La call me when he wakes up so I can have my moms bring the kids by."

"I'll be by when I leave here." Lala told her and she nodded her head before giving me one last look and then taking off in the direction of the exit.

I don't think I had ever felt as alone as I did in this moment. It was like I had no one and everyone was against me for being loyal and loving to my husband. Yeah, I knew I was wrong for not telling Lala but I didn't want to hear her mouth because she was riding with Mira way more than she was riding for me.

The shit Mira said about me and Lake not lasting stung a little bit. I had those same doubts, especially right after our last conversation about the baby, right before he got shot. When I heard those shots and saw him in all that blood all of my doubts went away and I knew that I had to be the woman he married, his rider.

"He did say that the baby wasn't his. He told her that he loved her and that he would never do anything like that to hurt her. Lake has been lying to you, he used you. I told you he would never leave her, you didn't listen. Now you've torn that family apart. Who's gonna explain this to those kids?" She stood before me. "And then you lied about all of this. I don't even know who you are." The disgusted look on her face stung my heart just a little and I let a few tears drop from my face.

"You don't know what you're talking about. He doesn't love her. He tells her what she needs to hear to make sure that he will still have a relationship with his kids. We were gonna tell her when the kids got a little older." I wiped my tears with the back of my hand. "But I see who you riding for."

"You dumb as hell if you believe that." I could hear the distaste rolling off of her tongue. Who the hell was the girl standing before me? She damn sure wasn't the girl that I call my friend. "It's not about who I'm riding for Miracle. I love you and you know that but right is right and wrong is wrong, simple as that and you," she pointed at me, "are dead ass wrong."

"I love him and he loves me," was the only thing that I could think to say because I knew that I was wrong for getting involved with a man who had a girl and kids but I couldn't help it. Lake told me that he didn't love her and that we were gonna be together so I believed him. If you ask me, he had one foot out the door before I even came into the picture. "I'm sorry we hurt her but I can't change how I feel and neither can he."

"Lake doesn't love you, you're just the young dumb chick that he knocked down and can get whatever he wants from, don't you see that?" She searched my eyes to see if what she was saying was registering with me and it wasn't.

She didn't see how it was. When we were together, we were made for each other. It didn't matter what anyone thought or how they felt about it, I knew what it was and that's all I was concerned with.

"You can leave." I sniffed back the tears. I turned my head to focus on anything but her, after a while she caught the drift and left.

After she was gone I was left there to wallow in my thoughts. I did something that I didn't want to do at a time like this. I began to doubt the relationship I had with Lake. I love that man and even though our marriage was unconventional, it was real.

As soon as he was well and talking we were gonna have a conversation about how he treated me when he found out about the baby and why they are saying he's not claiming the baby. I know that he was shocked at first but he had some explaining to do. That along with everything else that wasn't adding up at the moment.

Right now, I wasn't worried about that, I just needed my husband to pull through all of this. I put my head down in my lap and I prayed that God would have mercy on Lake and let him pull through this. I needed him, we needed him.

CHAPTER 3

*L*ala
My heart was heavy and my mind was clouded. So much shit was rolling through my brain that I was having a hard time deciphering it all. I needed Heart with me, I needed him here and he wasn't.

I didn't have anyone right now because Miracle had lost her got damn mind and Mira didn't know who she could trust but I didn't blame her. I would be looking at everyone sideways too.

What I wouldn't give to have Heart wrap his arms around me and tell me that everything would be okay even if it wasn't. I grabbed my phone out of my back pocket and hit the side button so that the screen lit up. I had to make sure that I didn't miss a call from Heart.

I was heading right down there to see what was going on as soon as I got an update on Lake. Miracle thought that because she had that piece of paper that it meant something. I didn't give a damn what she said, I was gone be right there whether she liked it or not.

Just then my phone rung and it was an unknown number, I hurried and answered it because I just knew that it was Heart. I hurried out the doors so that I could answer the call because my cell phone reception was sucky inside of the hospital.

"Hello!" I answered quickly.

"You have a collect call from an inmate at the Iredell County Correctional Facility, Heart, if you would like to accept the charges please select the number five..." I hurriedly hit five and she gave me some directions on what to do next as far as adding money to my phone so that I could accept calls from him. I did what I was told as I waited for his voice to flow through the receiver.

"La?" his voice was deep and full of anger. I wished that I was there to ease his mind. I knew that he was feeling fucked up about Lake and I couldn't blame him. "How is he?"

"He's gonna be okay baby, I'm sure of it. He hasn't woke up but Dr. Smire said that there is brain activity so he's still in there but we're just waiting on him to wake up. The doctor did say that his body needed to heal so he wouldn't do anything to wake him up manually, he would just wait for him to come to on his own so his body will have time to heal."

"Damn!" he said and I could hear the hurt in his tone. I felt bad that he had to deal with this alone, hell I hated that I had to deal with it alone. We needed each other and it wasn't possible and it's killing me. "I wish I was there man damn."

"Baby what happened?" I asked him wondering why in the hell he was in there in the first place.

"I beat the fuck out of Mitch's bitch ass." He said through gritted teeth.

"Oh God," I was really starting to hate him. I was at the point where I wanted him dead. Call me heartless but he was causing more drama in my life than I cared to deal with.

"I can't really say too much more, you know they taping this shit."

"Yeah baby I know, so does it look like they gone set you a bond?" I asked hopeful.

"Ion know baby, shit was worse than me just fucking him up. A nigga gone need a lawyer for this bullshit. They trumping charges and shit but I ain't about to let that shit fly." His words came out cool and confident but I was worried and thinking the worse. "Don't worry baby, I'll be home soon."

The tears immediately started to flow down my face as I thought about the fact that I may not see him for a while. We had just got our shit together and here we are having to deal with this shit. On top of all of that, Lake, our brother is laying in the hospital and there wasn't shit we could do about it.

I sat there and listened to him tell me that everything was gone be okay but I didn't believe him. I didn't know what was gone happen. I needed someone who knew about this shit or had been through this. Darren, my dad's best friend. Him and my dad had hella pull so I know that he could look into this for me.

The one thing that I dreaded more than anything was having to face my mother but at this point I had to do what I had to do.

Right now, Heart needed me and I was gone put my pride to the side and ask for some help. I needed him home to help me through this.

My thoughts were interrupted by the automated bitch, "You have thirty seconds." I wanted to reach through the phone and pull her out but I sighed instead.

"La, keep ya head up. Steer clear of that nigga Mitch because if he touches you while I'm in here, the next charges I'll be getting are for murder." He gritted. "I love you and I'll see you soon." Before I could answer the phone went dead.

"That wasn't thirty seconds bitch." I said into the phone. I was angry, hurt and confused, the fucked-up part about all of it, I had to go through the shit alone.

As bad as I wanted to wallow in my sorrow, Heart and Lake needed me and I wasn't about to let them down even though I was gonna tear Lake a new one the minute he opened his eyes.

Married? How in the fuck could they be married and we not know it? I was damn sure gonna ask Heart if he knew about it. If he did that was some fuck shit and I was cussing his ass out too. That shit is wrong on so many levels.

I hated that shit for Mira, I wanted to be there for her but I didn't know if she would be receptive to my sympathy seeing as though I was the best friend of the person causing her all of the pain. Reaching out was a must though so I would just have to prepare myself for rejection.

I also needed to prepare myself to go and talk to Darren. I knew he was with my mom and even though this had nothing to do with her it had everything to do with her. If I was going to be dealing with him, she would be there and I had to get in the right headspace to be able to handle that.

"This little stuck up bitch, she's the reason for all of this," the revulsion rolling off of his tongue with every word he said made the hairs on the back of my neck stand up. I knew that if I didn't get away from him at this minute that things could get ugly. "Oh, don't look scared now, when I finish with your little boyfriend I'll make sure that you pay for all of this. You see what happened to your little friend laying in there fighting for his life? You might just be next."

All that fear that was building up quickly turned to anger as I turned around and spit in his face. I know that's one of the nastiest things that you could do to someone but I wanted to show him just how much I hated his very existence.

"Fuck you! You think you did something?" I snarled. "Lake is coming up out of this and Heart will be home sooner than you think and when they do." I shook my head and I could see the fear dancing around in his eyes.

"Nah Heart ain't coming home and I'll make sure of that!" he said wiping the spit that collected on the side of his face. "But I promise you gone pay for that shit little girl.

"Fuck you!"

"Who the fuck is that Mitch?" I heard someone coming barreling around the corner from where we were standing outside of the hospital.

"Don't worry about who I am. What you need to do is worry about what's gone happen to him when Heart gets out and comes for revenge for him shooting Lake." I growled and then turned to walk away.

I didn't have anything to say to either of them and the more I stood in front of Mitch the more I wanted to find a gun and blow his fucking brains out. I hated to say that I hated someone but I hated him with a passion and I couldn't wait until he was dealt with.

When I got far enough I pulled out my phone and ordered an Uber. Heart had the truck when he got locked up so I needed to go pick up the Impala so that I would have a way around. After the Uber got there I gave them directions and opted to sit in the back so that I wouldn't be forced to talk to anyone.

I had so much on my mind and I needed to see if Darren could help Heart out of this or if he could point me in the direction of who could.

Knock! Knock! Knock! I lightly knocked on the door of the apartment that I used to live in. I could hear someone on the other side moving around. My heart was beating and I was flooded with a host of different emotions, but right now I needed to keep them at bay because I needed Darren to get Heart out of this mess.

I wasn't exactly sure what he was still into but I knew that he knew a lot of people because my dad did and they were one in the same. I just hoped that he could be what I needed right now.

When the door open my mom stood before me with a sympathetic look on her face. I guarantee she already knew what happened because news traveled real fast in the hood. For a while we just stood there and stared at one another. She lifted her arms like she was about to embrace me only for her to drop them right back down by her side. I could see the uncertainty swaying in her eyes. She didn't know how to approach me.

I knew she wanted to console me, but she also knew that our relationship was tainted and a wrong move could deepen that. I was happy for that because I didn't know if I was ready for that.

I was hurt at the way she had been treating me since my dad died and the fact that it took a man to come in and change her for the better caused an aching in my heart that I couldn't quite explain. It was like I wasn't good enough for her to come out of what she was feeling.

My dad dying hurt her and I get that. Don't get me wrong I still felt that pain till this day. I just needed her to step into that void and she caused a bigger one. Right now, I just needed to know if they could be there for me with this Heart situation and we would figure out the rest later.

"Who is that Cynthia?" I heard Darren say from behind her. "We need to go and check on..." his words trailed off as his face came into my view. The smile that was battling to come through did and I couldn't help but smile.

I remember being a little girl and he would come over to the house and the minute he would walk in the door I was in his arms. He had me spoiled rotten and no one could tell him anything about his princess diva.

Just as quick as the happy memories came flushing into my

mind they left because just like my mother he turned his back on me when my dad died. He said that he couldn't take it and that he needed to get away. Not once did he call and check on me or anything, he just said fuck me just like my mother.

"I need your help. Heart is locked up and I need to get him out," I said. Fuck the formalities, I wasn't in the mood for any family reunions. I just needed them to help me then they can go on and do whatever the fuck they were doing while I was out here fending for myself, minus the help from Heart. My heart was so bipolar with this situation that I couldn't keep up with how I was feeling myself.

"We were just coming to check on you, we heard about Lake and Heart. Honey are you okay?" she reached out to touch me and I flinched. She drew her hand back and covered her mouth with it. "I'm so sorry Laurence." She let the tears she was holding in fall but they didn't phase me one way or another.

"Well evidently Mitch shot Lake and Heart did something and got himself in jail. I need you to look into it Darren. I know when my dad was alive you handled stuff like that for him. Cause when I got caught driving you were the one that went and handled it." That memory caused him to crack a smile.

My dad taught me to drive at the age of 12 and when I turned 13 I wanted to go to the store but no one would take me, so I took my dad's car and drove to the store but I got pulled over for rolling through a stop sign.

"Mitch?" Darren furrowed his eyebrows and clenched his jaw. I didn't know what his issue with Darren was but it didn't matter because I was sure that when Heart saw him he wouldn't be breathing long enough for anyone else to have a problem with him. "Have they set a bail yet?"

"No!"

"Aight well let me go see what I can do. I got a partner there and he looked out for me and Big L and I'm sure nothing's changed." He gave me a reassuring smile but I could see the hatred in his eyes for who I'm guessing was Mitch. I didn't know what that was about but as long as Heart was out from behind bars I was good with it. "I'll be back."

He grabbed his keys and came to where I was standing before he walked out the door he turned to kiss my mom and I had to turn my head. I wasn't used to seeing that. As far as I was concerned for the moment that was my mom and he was my uncle.

Don't get me wrong, I knew she wasn't going to stay single forever but damn my daddy's best friend? I don't know if I can deal with that. So many questions swarmed around my head. Were they dealing with each other while my dad was alive? I mean she loved him, right? She wouldn't do that? After what she did to me I don't know what she's capable of.

Once he was gone, the air got a little thicker. We were silent neither of us said a thing. Finally, I just turned around and started to leave. My mind wasn't in the right place to think about anything concerning this situation right now and to be honest I don't know if I would be open to having a conversation with her right now. Before I could she said something under her breath that caused me to stop moving. When she realized she had my attention she repeated what she said a little louder.

"I'm sorry." She sniffled I could hear her trying to hold back her tears.

I swung around to face her again, to make sure that I heard her correctly, "What?" I tried to keep my attitude at bay but it was hard.

"I'm sorry baby," tears slowly cascaded down her face and I so badly wanted to hug her and tell her that everything would be okay and that we would figure it out but I didn't know if that was true. "I stopped loving myself, and I couldn't find a way to love you through that," she cried.

My heart was screaming for me to forgive her but my mind wouldn't allow me to forget the horrible things I went through after my dad died. It wouldn't let me let go of the hurt that she caused when she checked out on me. I was so confused.

All I needed right now was for Lake to wake up and Heart to be in my arms helping me through all this pain. I couldn't tell my mom what she wanted to hear right now so I walked close to her and leaned in and kissed her cheek, then looked her in the eyes and left.

Me and my mother would definitely have to have a sit down but right now wasn't the time. I needed to be there for Heart and Lake because that's who's been there for me!

CHAPTER 4

*D*arren
I've never wanted to get away from somewhere as fast as I did when I was standing in that room with Lala and Cynthia. I can remember when things used to be so simple and good with all of us. Big L made that happen. When he died it took a lot out of all of us and even though it effected Lala the most, me and Cynt took it the worst, if that makes sense.

I left because I couldn't take being here without Big L, that nigga was my brother and blood couldn't make us closer. When he got gunned down right in front of us, that shit took something out of me and there were no words to explain how hurt I felt. I still remember that day.

"Ayyyeee it's my baby girls birthday!" I yelled walking in Big L's house and greeting Lala. She was so beautiful with her skin the color of toasted almonds and her long dark hair flowing

down her back. She was the spitting image of her father with her mother's round face.

"Hey Uncle D, where's my present?" she wrapped her hands around my neck and squeezed for dear life. I embraced it because she was the closest thing to a child that I would ever have. I didn't want kids because of the line of work that we were in, that and the fact that I never stayed with no woman long enough to procreate.

"What you talking about present? I am your present, in the flesh." She quickly removed her hands and slipped them on her hips.

"Uncle D, now I know you playing." The cutest little smirk formed on her face and it caused a smile to appear on mine.

"Go outside." I whispered just as Cynthia walked in the living room with her hands on her hips and a dish towel hanging from her right

hand. I knew she was about to go off and for more reasons than one.

"Do y'all know what time it is and where is Lawrence?" she fussed. I was not about to get into this with them so I pointed to the door letting her know that he was outside. I heard Lala scream and I knew that she had already been introduced to her present. "Why would y'all buy her something so dangerous?" She scolded.

"That's what she asked for." I shrugged and she scoffed and headed in the direction of Big L and La. I laughed because she knew that deep down she had no say so over what Big L bought for his daughter and especially on her birthday.

I followed Cynthia outside and right when we got to the porch I noticed a blacked-out Impala sitting up the street. Lala and Big L were walking around his truck admiring the pink and black four-wheeler she requested for her birthday. Before I could get anyone's attention the car came rushing down the road.

"Big L watch out." I yelled as I jumped off the porch in the direction of Lala who was standing in the line of fire. Gun shots erupted and screams were resonating through the air. Everything seemed to go in slow motion, I watched as Big L tried his best to make it to Cynthia to protect her from the gun fire but the closer he got to the porch the more hits he took and before I knew it he was on the ground and Cynthia was screaming.

"Nooooo Lawrence! Noooooooo!"

"Da—daddy!" Lala said from underneath me as I tried my best to shield her from the sight before us but she was persistent and wiggled her way from under me. I immediately jumped up and made sure that it was safe before I let her go to her father.

"Fuck!!!!" I yelled out. As I stood over a struggling Big L, he was covered in blood and beginning to cough up blood. "Somebody call the fucking ambulance!" I yelled out to his nosey ass neighbors.

"I—I love y'all," Big L struggled to get out.

"Nah man don't fucking do that shit." I cussed at him. "You hear that? The ambulance is on its way." One of them must had called when they heard the shots. "Come on Big L, look stay with me brother."

"Daddy please, please don't leave me!"

"Baby we need you, I need you!" Cynthia cried, she cradled his head in her lap and rubbed his head.

"T—ta—ke care of th—em D, the mon—ey...." Was the last thing I heard before his eyes closed and his chest stopped rising up and down.

"Wh—what just happened?" Cynthia said with her hands up like she was surrendering. "Lawrence, wake up baby, don't fucking do this!" She screamed as loud as she could.

"Nooooo daddy daddy daddddddddyyyyyyy!" Lala screamed over and over.

The paramedics rushed over to where we were and began to work on him. They kept shocking him and pressing on his chest and nothing. We watched as they did everything that they could to no avail. When they brought the sheet out to pronounce his death Lala lost it. They ended up having to take both her and Cynthia to the hospital and things just went down from there. I just didn't think they would get this bad.

After Big L's funeral our connect asked me to take over for him and I couldn't do it. Call me a coward or whatever you want to but these were Big L's streets and I couldn't see myself doing this without him. So, I left. I know that I was wrong for just up and leaving but I wasn't in the mind frame to worry about anyone but myself.

I never thought that Cynthia would fall the way she did. I thought that if anything it would bring them closer together but I was wrong, dead ass wrong. Now that I was back I felt like shit that I wasn't there for them like Big L asked me to but I put it on everything that I was gone make up for that shit starting with helping Heart out of this shit. If anything, he's been the only person there for Lala and she deserves to have him with her.

Failure filled my soul as I set out on a mission to help clear this shit up. I know Big L is turning over in his grave right now.

Walking into the police station I caught a few stares from some of the officers who knew who I was. I could see the nervousness in their eyes and it bought a satisfactory feeling in the pit of my gut. They all knew that if I wanted to I could end their very existence in more ways than one.

Big L always made sure to keep insurance on any one that could possibly take us down and when I left town so did the insurance. I never knew when I would need it again so I kept it close.

"Detective Ringo please." I said to the lady cop who was sitting there like she wanted to tear me to pieces. I smiled at her but that's all she would be getting from me. My situation was complicated enough right now.

"He's in his office, let me ring him up." She inadvertently ran her tongue over her bottom lip, then tucked it between her lips. A few moments later he was walking through the squad room with a smile on his face and his arms spread open.

"What's up D? Man damn, where the hell you been?" He pulled me in for a brotherly hug.

"Shit was all bad, I had to get away." I told him referring to Big L dying, he nodded his head that he understood. "But I need to holla at you about something."

He nodded his head and headed back towards where he had just come from. When we got in there he shut the door and made his way behind the desk that sat in the middle of the room. I chose to stand.

"What's up man?"

"Heart Strong. I need him out of here." I looked him straight in the eyes. For a while we just had a stare off but Allen knew me, he used to be on our payroll so he knew how I could get down but I never had an issue with him helping us out.

"Damn," he said under his breath as he typed away on his computer. He sat back on his seat and began to rock back and forth. "Shit don't look good." He tilted his head and gave me his attention.

"What you mean?"

"Mitch, that nigga seems to be untouchable and shit. I been after his ass since he killed my fucking partner and every time I think I got something he slips through my fingers. The way they got ya boy hemmed up, Mitch got something to do with why he still here." He clicked a few more times and then a smirk went across his face. "Chief Shriel."

"Oh, that's it." It was my turn to smile as I pushed a few buttons on my phone and then I turned the phone in the direction of Allen. "That won't be a problem."

"Oh shit." he said before he began to laugh. I had pictures of him with multiple prostitutes, women and men, and I had proof that he paid for it. "Well, let me see what I can do." He said between laughs.

"What's his email?" I asked, he rattled it off and I sent him the pictures with a message saying that Heart Strong needed to be released by end of the day from a fake email address that I got from this spoofing software that I installed on my phone. "Done."

"So, what the fuck you need me for?"

"To find out whose name I needed to dirty up a little." I smirked. "So, what's the deal with this Mitch nigga anyway? Seems like everybody is after that nigga. The minute I stepped on NC soil that's all I've heard about and then he shot Lake and now Heart's after him."

"He killed my partner," he looked down and then looked back up at me. "You know I never stopped looking for Big L's killer. I sent my partner to look into a lead and it ended up at a warehouse that he runs."

"Say what now?" I could feel my blood began to boil and my fist clenched involuntarily. "Who is this nigga?"

"He works for Wyndel, he's married to his daughter." The look that he gave me showed me just how complicated this situation could get if it wasn't handled the correct way.

"Fuck, maybe I should have stayed where the fuck I was." I said more to myself than to anyone else.

I had ran into to Wyndel since I had been back and he told me that he had a job for me but I told him that I wasn't interested. Right now, I just wanted to make sure that I made up for my absence in Lala and Cynthia's life. Everything else would have to wait.

Me and Allen talked a little bit more, he told me what had been going on around town and how things had changed. Shit was way different than when me and Big L ran shit and from the looks of it I knew exactly what job Wyndel had for me.

"So how did it go?" Cynthia asked the minute she walked in the door. The desperation in her tone made me feel bad for her. She genuinely felt horrible about how she's treated La and she wanted to do what she needed to do to fix their relationship but at this point I didn't know if anything but time would help.

"He's getting processed out, all charges will be dropped because of a," I tried to think of the right thing to say without telling her how things went down, "technicality."

I had an email before I left Allen's office saying that he would be out and he wanted to see if we could meet up and he would pay me for the pictures. I laughed at the email and deleted the address from the spoofing app. I wasn't selling shit, these were going to come in handy. That much power over someone excited me.

"Oh, thank you." She threw her arms around my neck and let them linger and she told me thank you over and over again. My hands encircled her waist and rested right above her ass. When she brought her face up to mine she just stared into my eyes.

When I got here a few months ago and found her she was in bad shape. I helped her through a 90-day outpatient program and on her last day we went out and had dinner, then went back to her house. We drank, me Hennessy and her tea, and talked about old times and one thing led to another and the next morning we woke up in bed together feeling guilty.

We said that it wouldn't happen again but that was a lie and I didn't know if it was our love for Big L that brought us closer but I had fallen for this woman and I didn't know how I felt about it. I didn't know how Big L would feel about it.

Right now, we were just seeing where things went and Lala's opinion about the situation would play a big part in how we moved. I just had to get her to be in the same room with us long enough to have a conversation. I owed her an explanation.

"Everything is gonna work out." I leaned down and kissed her lips and she returned the kiss.

"Thank you for everything." There was more meaning behind those words so I didn't say anything, I just crashed my lips against hers again and let her show me just how appreciative she was.

CHAPTER 5

*H*eart

   "Strong!" I heard the CO call out. I didn't even bother to turn around. The events from today put me in a head space that I desperately needed to get out of before I ended up doing something worse than I already have. "Strong!"

   Without saying a word, I turned to glare into the eyes of my next victim if he didn't fix his tone. The moment our eyes met his once aggressive demeanor vanished and was replaced with fear. He took a few steps back from the cell that I was currently in and chose his next words very carefully.

   "You're free to go." He said with diminished confidence and disgust.

   For a minute I thought that he was fucking with me but the look he gave let me know that I was indeed free to go. I didn't know what the fuck was going on but I wasn't about to sit around and second guess the shit. I had shit to do and people to handle.

Standing up, I ran my hands down my face and the first person that came to mind was Lala. The last time I talked to her she sounded like she wasn't handling this shit too well but she tried to put on a brave act for me. I hated that I ran off of emotions and left her to deal with all of this shit herself.

When I got to the opening of the cell the CO opened it so that he was standing behind it like that would somehow save him from what I was feeling at the moment. I walked out the cell and just turned around to stare at him. The way his lip quivered at the mere thought that I might touch him made my dick hard but I had more pressing issues to deal with.

"If you ever talk to me like that again," I started and he reached for his gun, "you think I give a fuck about that gun?" I said through gritted teeth.

The anger and hurt that I was feeling about everything that was going on right now trumped any reason that I should have housed at the moment. The only thing standing in the way of me touching his punk ass was the fact that Lala needed me and so did Lake.

After a long ass stare down I turned to allow him to shut the door and show me where I needed to go. Before he could do that, we were joined by some old ass white nigga with a big ass beer gut, he was dressed in a suit and wore a tight ass mug on his face. I had a feeling that this conversation wasn't about to be good and I was already on the defense.

"I got this Todds." He told the scary ass CO. "Follow me," he addressed me and for a minute I just stood there and when he realized I wasn't behind him he stopped with his back to me. "To get out of here you need to follow me."

With that he continued to walk, I needed to get the fuck out of here so against my better judgement I went with him. He led me to an office where he held the door open until I walked in and he shut it.

"What the fuck is this about? I ain't no snitch so I ain't telling you shit." I slipped my hands in my pants.

"You think I give a fuck about you telling me anything?" My fist balled up in my pockets. "You must know some really powerful people, to pull off the shit that you did to get you out of here."

"What the fuck are you talking about?" Confusion filled my mind.

"That's the fucking problem with you niggers." He spat, as I took a step towards his desk that he was now standing behind. "I don't know who you think you are or what you think you know but if you ever threaten me again Mitch will be the least of your worries."

At just the mention of his name everything in me turned cold and pure hatred flushed my veins and before I knew it I was behind that desk with his dress shirt in my hands and his feet were off the ground.

"I don't take too kindly to threats, clearly you don't fucking know me because if you did you would watch who the fuck you were talking to." I said through gritted teeth.

"I'm the chief of police, if you do something to me in here it will be the end of your very existence."

"Again, I don't take too kindly to threats." I shoved him back and he landed on his ass and I stood over him. "You must be one of Mitch's bitches."

"That's neither here nor there just tell whoever you got working for you to keep my personal life out of your thugged out bullshit," he growled. "If y'all want to kill each other be my guest but leave my career out of it."

I was confused about what the fuck he was talking about, I didn't threaten him or his whack ass career but I would end his life if he kept fucking with me. I didn't have time to keep dealing with this shit.

Turning around I headed for the door but he stopped me, "How much for the pictures?" I turned to him as he was picking himself up off the ground.

"What the fuck are you talking about?" I glared at him.

"You can pretend all you want to but everyone has a price, I'll be in touch." He brushed his suit off and sat in his seat like nothing had ever happened. He never looked up again. I didn't know what the fuck was going on but I needed to find the fuck out.

Exiting the police station an hour later, it took them that long to give me my shit. I reached for my phone that I had slid in my pocket. I powered it on but got nothing. I shook my head at my luck at the present moment. I looked out into oncoming traffic and noticed the convenience store with the barbecue place attached to it. Maybe they would let me use the phone because I refused to go back in that muthafucka I just walked out of.

"Heart!" I could hear calling out behind me but I was determined to get away from where I was so I kept it moving. "Heart! Do you need a ride?" I ignored her, I didn't even have to turn around to see who the fuck it was. Now was not the time to be getting caught up in her bullshit.

"Aye you think I can use the phone?" I asked the clerk behind the counter. She was semi cute but she thought she was the shit, hence the reason she was currently licking her lips at me.

"What will I get out of it?" she said and gave me a toothless smile, a nigga had to jump back because I wasn't expecting that.

"Not a got damn thing, you should be worried about checking out a dentist and not worrying about someone's man." Quinia popped her gum as she rushed into the store as the clerk was attempting to flirt with me.

"Bitch I don't know who you talking to with those run-down Converse, you got some nerve." She rolled her eyes at Quinia who was currently looking down at the shoes she had on her feet. I wasn't really impressed by the catty fight they were having I just wanted them both to shut the hell up so I could figure out how in the hell I was getting the fuck away from here. "Do you need to use the phone because there is no way that your fine ass is associated with this bitch." She held the cordless phone in my direction.

I took it from her and walked off to the side of the counter to try and call Lala, while the two of them continued to go back and forth with each other. After the fourth attempt I gave up on calling Lala. I handed the clerk her phone back and thanked her and headed out to the parking lot to try and catch a cab or something.

I reached for my wallet because I knew I had at least a g with me when that shit went down but when I pulled out my wallet it was empty as fuck. "Dirty bastards!" I yelled out.

"Look, let me give you a ride home." Quinia said walking out of the store and in my direction. I shook my head because the last thing I needed right now was for Lala to see me with her and some shit pop off. I already had enough on my plate and I didn't need this shit right now. "Damn it ain't like we fucking, hell that little bitch will live if I give you a ride home."

I rushed her so fast and had the little cut off shirt she had on balled up in my hands and her on her tiptoes trying to keep control of her balance. I don't know what she don't understand right, she was not about to disrespect Lala, no one was and damn sure not in my presence.

"Call her out her name again and I swear you won't live to tell about it." I said through gritted teeth.

"All I was trying to say is it's just a ride, no strings." Her chinky eyes were stretched to capacity, I don't think I ever seen her eyes that wide before. I could see the fear swinging around them but I had warned her on more than one occasion about disrespecting La and she didn't listen. "I was just trying to help damn."

I slowly let her go and sat her to her feet. My anger was all over the place and I couldn't control it, I could seriously snap at any minute and seriously hurt someone.

"Yo take me to the hospital and I ain't trying to hear about this shit." I said against my better judgement. I had a feeling that I was gone regret this shit but right now I needed a ride the fuck out of here.

"Come on." Was all she said. Quinia was still the desperate bitch that she's always been. She thinks I'm stupid but I know she's just looking for a reason to be near me and throw that shit in Lala's face.

She led the way to her sisters car, I didn't even realize that it was sitting there. I slid in the passenger seat and immediately plugged my phone up to the car charger. The minute it was charged enough to use I called Lala immediately.

"Baby!" she yelled, I could hear the worry in her voice and I was almost afraid to ask what was going on. I hated to hear her like that. "I'm so glad Darren came through, it's the least he could do seeing as though he left me high and dry when dad died." The sadness in her voice pissed me off but I was trying to keep it together.

"Darren huh?" I knew what him and Big L was in back in the day, I needed to holla at him about a few things and soon but first I needed to check on Lala and Lake.

"Where are you? Do you need me to come pick you up?" I sighed heavily because one thing that I told myself that I wouldn't do is to lie to her. Because I need this to work, we need us to work.

"I caught a ride from someone coming that way, so I'll be there shortly. I'm headed straight to the hospital so just meet me there." I said trying to get her mind off of who was bringing me there.

"I'm already here," she said sadly.

"Why you sound like that baby?" My heart sank to my chest, a part of me didn't want to hear what was about to come out of her mouth but I needed to know.

"He still won't wake up," I could hear her trying to hold back the tears. "I need you." She finally let the tears go.

"Baby I'm on my way," I assured her. "Aye, I love you aight?"

"I love you too," she said through her sniffles.

I attempted to calm her down. I knew I should have told her who I was with but I didn't want to make the situation worse than what it was. I glanced over at Quinia and she had a smirk on her face. I shook my head and focused my attention on the window, I just prayed that she didn't start her bullshit but I should have known better than that.

"So why didn't you tell her that I was the one that gave you a ride?" The humor in her tone pissed me off.

"Did you tell your sister that you're giving me a ride?" I turned my attention to her and her bright skin took on a red hue that gave me the satisfaction that I needed in that moment.

"I don't understand why you do me like this Heart. I've been good to you, I'm always there when you need me like now. Where was everybody else when you needed them? Where was your precious Lala?" She vented.

"Quinia, that's where you fuck up at." I wasn't in the mood to be handing out life lessons but the bitch seemed like she needed it and maybe it would help her get the notion that I wanted anything to do with her out of her head. "I never asked you to do shit for me but swallow my dick and take it from time to time, that's it. I never once gave you any indication that we were gonna be more than that. You made up this whole relation-ship that you wanted with me in your mind, that shit ain't my fault. How I felt for you is how I treated you, that should tell you something in itself."

She was quiet for a minute, like she was trying to process what I had just said. I had hope for her, but only for a second. When she started to speak again I knew that there was no hope for her.

"You never gave me a chance to be what Lala is to you. I could have been that Heart. Like what makes her so much better than me? Huh?"

"Quinia I ain't about to teach no grown ass woman how to be a woman. Ya mama should have done that." I shook my head. "I just clowned you about sleeping with ya sister and you don't even give a fuck, you willing to sweep that shit under the rug just to be with me? That lets me know you have no respect for your-self, and you damn sure don't know your worth."

"I handled that and it won't happen again. My sister was just mad at her baby daddy at the time and now they are back together and we won't even have that problem anymore." The confidence she had in what she just said made me hate the day I ever started fucking with her.

"You missed the whole point, I fucked your sister because I didn't give a fuck about you or your feelings about it. You don't mean shit to me. I would never do no shit like that to Lala because I love her and I respect her too much. Plus, she's more than enough woman for me. She got goals, she's in school to do something with her life. That's the kind of woman that I want on my team." I said with so much conviction that I scared my damn self. "I could never see myself settling down with someone who has, hell who still is fucking every baller that rolls through King's Creek apartments."

"Everybody has a past." Was her response.

"Yeah and everybody has a future, mine just doesn't include you."

With that I turned to the window and got so lost in my thoughts that I didn't even realize that I we had pulled up to the hospital until I heard Quinia open her mouth.

"Well there goes little miss perfect and she doesn't look happy." Humor masked the hurt that I could hear in her voice. What I said must have sunk in because she was not upset. I didn't give a fuck either way, I had to do damage control and fast.

Hopping out of the car before Lala could get there, I ran up to her and she swung on me. I ducked and barely missed the hit.

"Chill baby it ain't what you think." The look she gave told me that I had just a few seconds to explain myself before she flip the fuck out.

CHAPTER 6

*L*ala

       With everything going on around us he comes pulling up with this bitch. The way I was feeling we were about to be switching roles because I was about to be in jail for fucking the both of them up. Now he was sitting here talking about it ain't what you think. The last time I told him that he turned his back on me and acted like a straight bitch.

"I called you like four times and you didn't answer," he looked at me and I opened my mouth to say something but he held his hands up to stop me. "Nah cause we got too much going on to be fighting over bullshit. Yeah, I shouldn't have got in the car with her but at the time I didn't have a fucking choice. I needed to get home to you and to check on Lake." He took a step towards me and I took a step back. "I didn't have any cash on me to catch a cab because them pussy ass cops took all of my fucking money. She was there at the store. I didn't call her or ask her to come she was just there."

The honesty in his tone made me feel a little better about the situation but the fact that he found himself in her presence annoyed me and I wanted him to know that. One thing that I wasn't about to do is continue to go back and forth with this bitch about my man, Heart needed to handle that shit and fast.

"Damn chill I brought him back." She said through a crack in the window. I gave her one look and that bitch hit that lock so quick. "I mean damn I just borrowed him, I missed that big ol' thang." She laughed and I thought I was gone blow a gasket. I took a step towards her but Heart threw his arm up to block me.

"Quinia keep that shit up and I'mma fuck you up. You know what it is." Heart said in an even tone. The humor that was dancing around in her eyes was no longer there and it was replaced with fear.

I looked back and forth between the two of them and stepped back. Heart looked like he wanted to object but he just let me be and I was glad about that because I didn't feel like arguing with him. The way I saw it, he was just as much to blame as her.

Shaking my head, I slipped my hands in the back pocket of my jeans and walked in the opposite direction of where we were standing. I didn't want to sit there and argue with her or anyone else. I had too much shit going on and I wasn't about to feed in to her negative energy.

"Lala!" Heart yelled out but I kept walking until I felt myself being jerked back. "I know you heard me calling you, too much shit going down for you to be acting like a fucking brat." I watched his chest heave up and down. He was pissed but I didn't have any sympathy for him at this moment. "You didn't answer the fucking phone La what did you want me to do? Walk the fuck from Statesville? I didn't have the money to get a fucking cab and my phone was dead so I couldn't order a Uber. So please fucking explain what the fuck you wanted me to do!"

"I wanted you to do exactly what the fuck you did, get in the car with the bitch you were fucking before me and start more drama than we were already fucking dealing with. That's what the fuck I wanted you to do Heart."

He dropped his head and sighed heavily. "Only thing going through my head was getting back down here to you so that we can get through this shit together. I don't give a fuck about that bitch. I don't know how many times I got to tell you that I don't want that bitch. If I wanted to fuck her I could have pulled over on side of the road and handled that before I got here to you and you would have never known anything about it. You think that bitch running her mouth because we fucking? Hell no! She mad because I ain't blessing her, can't you see that?"

"I never said anything about you fucking her, it's still disrespectful as fuck and if I let the shit fly you will think that shit is cool and before I know it I'm gone be sitting somewhere like Mira. Riding for a nigga, having his kids all the while he out here fucking bitches and getting married." I yelled and couldn't stop the tears that flowed down my face. I knew it wasn't fair to lay their problems on him but I couldn't help it because I didn't want what was happening to Mira to happen to me.

"What the fuck are you talking about?" Heart took a step

towards me and closed the gap that I had created. "First don't compare me to no nigga, I don't give a fuck who it is. I'm me and there is no comparison." His tone was even but the power in his words were clear. "And what the fuck are you talking about Lake married? I been knowing that nigga since we were youngins, he ain't married and I know that shit for a fact."

"Same thing I thought about Miracle but she showed Mira and me their marriage license and they are indeed married." I crossed my arms across my chest and glared at him.

"Look that shit ain't got nothing to do with me or us. And I'm sure that there is an explanation for the shit you talking about and as soon as my nigga wake up he gone let y'all know what's up but for right now keep that shit between them and out of our shit." He demanded.

My eyes bore into his and I could see the hurt that he was feeling right now. My nigga was hurting and I was sitting here flipping about some irrelevant shit. I threw my arms around his neck and he encircled me in his arms.

"I love you so much." I cried.

"I love you too, always have and always will." He said as he pulled back to look at me. "Don't ever do that shit again, I know it's some fucked up shit going on but don't let that shit affect us. We better than that." He gave me a warning glare and I nodded my head.

"I just would rather you not be in that bitches presence if that's okay with you." Even though he said what he said, I still wanted him to know that him being around her bothered me. Call me childish, but I didn't trust that bitch no further than I could throw her and the bitch is thicker than me.

"You got that baby!" Was all he said and I believed him. He leaned down and kissed my lips and grabbed my hand and we headed in the direction of the hospital entrance.

When we got to the car, Quinia was still sitting there staring at us. I stopped right by the window and looked at her. I was sick of this bitch. You would think that ass whooping I gave her would have knocked some sense into her but clearly it didn't.

"I'm about over your shit, if I see you anywhere near my nigga again, you gone hate the day that I met you." I snarled my nose up at her and she rolled her eyes, crunk up the car and slowly backed up but not before giving us one last glance. I knew that I was gone have to fuck this hoe up again.

Heart intertwined our fingers and we walked in to check on our brother. We needed him to wake up and fix all this shit his ass started. I didn't know what was going on with him and Miracle but they both need a reality check. What they're doing is hurting Mira and will in turn hurt those babies. He needs to fix this.

"Damn I feel bad for sis," Heart shook his head and squeezed my hand. "I know Mira up here going crazy." I furrowed my brow and looked at him like he was going crazy. I jerked my hand back causing him to stop. I was about to cuss him out until the confusion on his face made me realize that he didn't have a fucking clue what was going on. "What the fuck is going on?"

"Shit I forgot you weren't here." I ran my free hand threw my hair that was hanging down my back. "Mira ain't here, Miracle is."

"Man, what the fuck?"

"Mira and Miracle was arguing and the doctor asked who would be making the decisions and Miracle whipped out the marriage license and told him that she would, that's how I found out about them being married. They fought and then Mira stormed out, I left and went to talk to Darren to help me with you and then I went to see her but she wouldn't let me in. I figured I would give her some space." I shrugged.

This shit was all fucked up, I swear I couldn't say that shit enough. Mira wasn't in the head space to deal with this alone but she wasn't in the mood to be around me. I get it, I mean Miracle was my best friend. I say was because I honestly don't know who the hell this girl is. I've never known her to act the way she's acting right now.

I just want everything to go back to the way it was before all hell broke loose. After I filled him in on everything that had happened we headed up to see Lake. I just hoped Miracle was off her high horse.

CHAPTER 7

M iracle

"Baby I need you to wake up." I choked up on my words. This has been the worse day of my life. I can't believe this shit happened to me. I was so confused on how to feel at the moment. A part of me wanted to be mad at him but the part that loves him wouldn't let me. "Why would you deny our baby, why would you deny your love for me? I know things are so messed up right now but that don't change the promise that we made to each other."

I broke down and cried on his chest where my head was laid. Doctor Smire came out and told me that I could come back a while ago. I messaged Lala and told her that we could go back and for her to tell Mira. No matter what the situation I would never try and keep her from being here, she's the mother of his children. So long as she keeps the bullshit at home we're good.

I never wanted to play the wife card but I wasn't about to let her tell me that I couldn't be here. After I got my cry out I stood up and walked over to the window, climbed in the window pane, pulled my knees to my chest and stared out the window.

Nobody understood the depths of our relationship, the things that we've done for each other. We were connected in a way that no one would ever compare to. There are some things that took place that got us to this point but it's more than that and no one could tell me any different.

I heard the door to the room slowly open up but I didn't bother to look towards the door. It was more than likely Lala and the fact that she had turned her back on me hurt me more than I would like to admit. Friends were never a thing on my priority list until I met La, we clicked immediately and we became more like sisters which is why her certain change in attitude towards me was baffling.

"Damn my nigga." I looked over the minute I heard the pain in Heart's voice. They were brothers and blood couldn't make them any closer. I knew this was fucking with him. I wandered what the hell was going on that would cause Mitch to shoot Lake. "I should've been there, we should've took care of that nigga that night in the club and you wouldn't be laying there.

"This ain't ya fault baby." Lala said standing by his side.

A tinge of envy slithered its way through my heart, that's what I wanted for me and Lake. The genuine, unconditional love that can make it through anything. The kind of love that you aren't ashamed of, one that you don't want to hide. Like I said before, Lake and I's love was unconventional but it was real, it's just sometimes I wish it was black and white, like theirs.

"Nigga you need to wake yo ass up." Hearts voice was stern. "You gotta get up and fix this shit with Mira, you got her worried and fucked up over this marriage shit. What the fuck were you thinking man?" I could see the lone tear roll down his face. "I'mma help her ass fuck you up when you get the hell up out of here."

"I'm sitting here." I finally opened my mouth.

"What the fuck is going on Miracle, when the fuck did y'all get married?" Heart asked. "Do it got anything to do with that night?"

"What night?" Lala interjected looking back and forth between me and Heart. "Hello! What night?"

Tears immediately filled my eyes as I thought about the night that I almost lost my life.

"All you got to do is go hand him the bag and he gone give you the money." Lake said from the passenger side of his beat-up Honda Accord.

Him and Heart had to go to a meeting that Mitch was having and they couldn't miss it but he had a sale that he didn't want to miss either. So, I volunteered to help him out, at first, he was against it but I assured him that I would be fine, it wasn't like this was the first time that I had done it. I used to run for my mom's boyfriend all the time to get extra money in my pockets.

After convincing him that I was very capable of doing this he dropped the drugs off to me at my apartment. The drop was at the top of the creek so it wasn't like I would have to go far.

"I know how to do this Lake." I rolled my eyes. "Just make sure that you come make this up to me when you're done." I smirked at him.

"I should have never let yo young ass sample the dick." He leaned over and kissed my lips and rubbed my pussy through my tiny cotton shorts.

"See and it's shit like that that got me hooked." I bit my lip and leaned over the seat and pressed my lips against his. "You sure you ain't got time to handle this?"

I grabbed his hand that was still between my legs and pressed it further into the puddle that he had just created. He slid my shorts to the side and slipped one of his fingers into my goodness causing me to moan against his lips.

"Damn girl!" He whispered as he continued to play in my wetness.

All of a sudden, he removed his hands and began to work his ball shorts down his long legs. I smirked because he could never deny me no matter how hard he tried, our connection was just that strong.

Leaning over I took his semi hard dick into my mouth and lightly sucked until he was at his full potential. Taking him to the back of my throat, I began to aggressively bob my head up and down his shaft.

Lake was the first dick that I had ever sucked, I caught him slipping when I was 17 and he showed me how to please him. He wouldn't fuck me because I was under age but he did let me give him head. So, if there was one thing that I knew how to do, that was to satisfy Lake.

"You gone make me nut, fuck." He grabbed my hair and pulled my head back so that I was looking up into him. For a minute he just stared at me and then he kissed me hard and nasty just how I liked it. *"Handle this shit."* He said against my lips and without another word I climbed over the seat as he laid it back and I straddled his lap.

"Ummm fuck baby." I cried out as I tried to fit all of him in me. Lake was the only man that I had been with sexually and I was still getting use to him.

"Show me something." He taunted.

Rolling my hips back and forth making sure to grind on him just how he taught me. He bit his lip and threw his head against the headrest and watched me do my thing. I rolled and bounced like my life depended on it.

The moans and the way he gripped my thighs let me know that he was enjoying the way I was handling what was mine. His phone rang against the floor board of the car but he ignored it.

"Do you need to get that?" I slowed down my motions but Lake slid down a little so that he could stroke me from underneath and that made me forget about his phone.

I could feel the orgasm traveling to the pit of my stomach causing me to shiver. *"Umhmmm let that shit go baby I feel it. Cum with me."* His voice was low and husky.

"Oh, shit baby, yessss oh god yes! It feels so good." I threw my head back and rode the wave of ecstasy as I brought myself and Lake to a much-needed orgasm.

"Got damn Miracle, yo shit is dangerous as fuck!" He said

lifting me up and putting me on my side of the car. "You keep on and you gone make a nigga crazy."

"Crazy enough to leave your girl?" I didn't look at him when I said it because I knew what was coming. His relationship with Mira was a sensitive subject with us and I didn't want to ruin the moment so I decided to take it somewhere else. "You wanna come in and wash off before you have to go to your meeting."

He didn't say anything he just looked at me and released a frustrated sigh. He was annoyed with what I had just asked but it was a legitimate question on my end, but a sticky one on his. I decided to let it go so hopefully this wouldn't turn into a fight.

"Nah I gotta go but I'll holla at you later." He pulled up his shorts and then stared out the front window and didn't say anything else.

"You not coming back later?" I asked after an uncomfortable silence.

"I'll holla at you later." He said with finality.

I could feel the tears welling up in my eyes but I willed them not to fall. "I'll text you after I meet up with bug and them." Was all I said as I climbed out of the car and then grabbed the bag out of the back of the Honda.

After I shut the door I just stood there and watched him pull off. Every time I brought up Mira he would get this cold demeanor and attitude. A part of me thought that maybe I should just walk away from him but I loved him too much so I didn't, that and the fact he told me that in the end it would just be me and him.

I shook my head and made my way in my apartment, it was

almost my birthday and me and Lake had plans to ride out to Virginia and spend the week at the beach, now that he was in his feelings I don't know if that would be happening.

I threw the bag on the couch and headed to the back to shower and change my clothes. Right when I got to the back of my apartment I heard a knock on the door. I couldn't help the smile that spread across my face because I just know that it was Lake coming back to tell me that he was sorry for how he acted, that's how it always went down. He could never stay mad at me.

"Did you change your mind about that sh—" my words were cut off by the butt of a gun coming down on my nose. I looked in the eyes of the masked man and began to cry. "Who the fuck are you and what do you want?" I screamed and he pushed me back into the apartment and shut the door.

"Where the drugs at?" I had a feeling that's what this was about.

"What drugs? I don't know what you talking about." I cried even harder and he put the gun to my head.

"Keep playing with me bitch, where the fuck are the drugs?" He said through gritted teeth. His breath reeked of cigarettes and booze, making my stomach hurt. "I ain't gone ask you again."

Before I could say anything, the door opened and Lake came in blasting, the guy took two to the back of the head. The masked man ended up falling on top of me, I started to scream.

"Chill baby, it's me. You okay?" He rolled the dude off of me and helped me off of the ground. When I was up on my feet he pulled me into him and hugged me. "I'm so sorry baby, fuck I'm sorry."

He pulled me back and stared into my eyes, he looked me up and down making sure there wasn't a scratch on me. That small gesture made me fall in love with him even more. He loved me more than he voiced.

"I'm okay baby, I'm good." I tried to reassure him but he shook his head.

"Nah I should have never put you in this shit, that's on me." I could see the regret in his eyes, it made me feel bad for him. "Look, don't you ever tell no one about this okay? I could get in a lot of trouble so I need you to forget this." He raised his brow.

"You don't have to tell me that Lake, I know the streets." I jerked away from him.

"Look I'mma call Heart to help me clean this shit up, go shower and put the clothes you got on in a bag. I'm sure no one called the police, hell this the hood, they know better."

I nodded my head and headed back to the bathroom to do what I was told. From that moment on Lake and I had been stuck like glue. It was like we saved each other in a sense.

"Yo Miracle?" Heart yelled at me and I snapped my head to meet his stare.

"That night has nothing to do with how we feel about each other." I said with so much conviction and Lala's stern demeanor relaxed just a little but it didn't last.

"WHAT NIGHT?" She yelled so loud that the nurse came around the corner to see what was going on. After I waved them off and then looked at her as Heart began to give her the short version of what happened that night.

"That night doesn't mean shit, Lake knew how loyal I was to

him. He didn't have to marry me to keep me quiet, I never would have said anything. He knows it and so do you." My voice raised a few octaves as I slid off the window seal to face them both. "Lake married me because he loved me not because he murdered someone to save my life. Whether you believe it or not what we have is real."

"Miracle I can't believe you are this naïve, I never took you as that chick. Since I've known you, you have been so carefree, independent and strong. Like I look up to the way you carried yourself. Never would I have ever thought that you would be out here looking dumb. That man don't love you, he fucking did that shit so you wouldn't ever open your mouth about anything." She shook her head and threw me a look of pure disgust. "I never took you for a dumb broad."

"You know what La? I don't know what the fuck your problem is with me right now but I'mma let that shit slide because of the situation but I won't take too much more of your disrespect." I said in a warning tone. "For your information spousal privilege only applies to what he tells me, I was there so that shit don't even matter."

"I'm sure Lake didn't know that, or he wouldn't have married you. He loves Mira and their kids, you were just something to pass the time. Wake up girl! You done stepped in and ruined this family and you don't even give a fuck. I feel sorry for you when Karma comes around and bites you in the ass."

"You can get the fuck out Lala, I got too much shit going on to even deal with this!"

"I ain't going nowhere, I ain't Mira! I'll beat your ass and think nothing of it! Try to get me put out of here from seeing Lake and see what the fuck happens. I love you with every ounce of love in me but you doing some fucked up shit right now and you can't even see that shit."

I didn't bother to say anything else to her or Heart, I climbed back in my window sill and watched the cars drive past the hospital. I said a prayer to God to let him come out of this. They stayed for a little while longer, Heart got an update from the doctor and then the two of them left without another word to me.

Once they were gone I was lost again in my thoughts. Lala's words were slowly inching their way into my mind and heart. Has Lake been lying to me? Nah, there is no way things would be like they are if he didn't love me. His actions spoke for themselves. Shaking the negativity out of my mind, I climbed out of the window right as a pain shot through my stomach reminding me that I hadn't ate.

"I'll be right back baby." I told Lake as I reached for the door to go to the cafeteria to see what they had to eat today. "What the fuck!" I yelled out as I ran right into someone.

When I looked up it was the chick that showed up at Waffle House that night we left the party at DLo's house.

"Why are you here?" She sneered

"He's my husband why in the fuck wouldn't I be here? Why the fuck are you here?" My hands found my hips and I was ready to give her a piece of my mind.

"Married? Lake is not married and if he is, he married the bitch who birthed his kids not you." She said more confident than I would have liked. It was like she knew something about Lake that I didn't.

"You can leave now, it'll be over my dead body if you get anywhere near my husband. You can say what you want but facts are facts! NURSE!" I yelled.

"Mrs. Childs, is everything okay?" The nurse ran around the corner and approached us.

"No everything is not okay, I want her away from here and she is not to be anywhere near my husband again!" I said right before I walked back in the room. "Damn it Lake!" I yelled before I burst out crying, this baby had me way too emotional but then again, this whole situation was enough to drive anyone crazy.

I sat in the chair that was beside his bed and cried myself to sleep. This shit was really taking a toll on me.

CHAPTER 8

M ira

       I could literally feel my heart breaking with the thoughts of him being to her what he was to me. That was supposed to be me with his last name, me sitting right there beside him nursing him back to health. I've been with this man for seven years and I ended up being the side chick. How?

Racking my brain trying to figure out how in the hell this happened, how could he be married and I not know. My mind kept trying to drift into the thoughts that this was somehow my fault but I was confident in the woman that I was. I did everything that I could to make that man happy, clearly it wasn't enough but that's not on me.

"Well, well, well we got to stop meeting like this." I looked into the eyes of the chocolate god I met that day at the hospital the day my life was turned upside down.

"Mitch, right?" I asked and he smiled displaying a beautiful set of teeth. I found myself squeezing my legs together to keep from thinking about him the way that I was. I shook the thoughts out of my head because I was already in a fucked-up situation behind a man and I wasn't trying to go there again.

Lake had my trust and thoughts behind men all fucked up and I told myself the minute I walked out of that hospital, that once I got my closure on this situation that I was going to focus on me and my kids and I put that on my life. I loved that man more than I should have but I was done. Him marrying that bitch was the ultimate sign of disrespect, he gave her everything that he promised me and that's something that I couldn't get over.

There was no future for us and I knew it, and I wasn't about to force it. Getting into another relationship right now wasn't on the agenda either.

"Earth to Mira." Mitch said snapping me out of my thoughts and bringing my attention back to him.

"I'm sorry, what were you saying?" I blinked a few times to get myself back to reality.

"I said, this is the second time I've seen you sitting by yourself looking all sad." He raised his eyebrows waiting for an answer that he was never gonna get. Why I was upset was none of his business and I didn't plan on letting him into my thoughts. Something about this man screamed trouble and for once I was gonna listen to my gut.

"I'm just going through something," I released a nervous chuckle. "You know, just life stuff."

"I hope like hell it ain't behind no man." I scoffed and he

shook his head. "Whatever it is you don't deserve it. You're too beautiful and I can feel your spirit from here and it's pure. You're a good person and you deserve someone that's going to appreciate that." He smiled again and my clit thumped.

"Thanks." Was all I could think of to say.

"How about we get out of here and go hang out?" I looked around the empty bar. I came here after my mom came and got the kids earlier today. I went to the hospital but just seeing her sitting there with him did something to me and I had to leave. I was so tore up at the sight I came to the bar to have a few drinks before I went to an empty house to dwell in my sorrow.

"I don't think that's a good idea," I shook my head vigorously, more to convince myself. This is not what I needed right now no matter how bad I may have wanted to play the revenge card, that just wasn't who I was. "I'm going through something right now and being alone with a man while my mind is cloudy wouldn't be a good thing."

"For you or me?" leaning down so that we were face to face, he flashed a sly grin and I returned a smile. His presence was just that infectious, you couldn't help but relish in it.

"For either of us, I got too much going on and I ain't trying to add anything to that." I searched his eyes for understanding but I could tell that he wasn't about to take no for an answer so I went ahead and crushed his dreams so he would just leave. "And I'm not the kind of girl that fucks for sport, so that won't be happening."

Nodding his head slowly he leaned back and stood straight, slipping his hands in his pockets. For a while we just stood there in an uncomfortable silence. I took a minute to take in the scratches on his face that were there the day I met him. He was dressed to the nines in a teal colored polo that complimented his chocolate skin and the stone washed jeans the hung loosely around his waist outlined his slightly bowed legs. The man was fine, there was no doubt about that but my heart was too scarred to even think the thought.

"You're something special Ms. Mira, and you're worth the wait. I'll see you again, I can promise you that." He winked and backed away from the bar.

The way he said that sent chills up my spine, I hoped like hell he wasn't some stalker or no shit like that. Nah, he couldn't be, he's too fine for that. Nigga probably got pussy knocking his door down. I laughed at my own joke and then signaled for the bartender to bring me another long island.

Life for me was also fucked up and I couldn't fathom the thought of having to start over, learning someone new, getting to know someone all over again and I didn't even want to get started on my kids but I didn't have a choice. I couldn't be that woman who stood by a man that didn't give a fuck about her and Lake's actions clearly showed that.

All it took was for him to show me who he was and I was damn sure gone believe him. Trust was broken and, in my eyes, it could never be repaired. I just hoped when he came out of this he understood that. Because when it came down to it, he was the father of my twins and I wanted us to co-parent effectively, we didn't have to be together to do that.

My heart hurt for my kids, I couldn't even bring myself to

think how I would explain this to them. How do I tell them that daddy is a piece of shit who married a whore and he won't be living with us anymore? How do you explain that to five-year olds?

That shit has been plaguing my mind every day since Lake got shot, what do I say? *You decided to be with a little hoe and left us to the wayside.* The way my heart was set up, I wanted to hate him but I couldn't. There was one thing that I did know, and that's the fact that I was done being for him.

"Well look who it is?" That voice brought some kind of peace to my heart, and the smile that replaced the frown was inevitable. "Mira Mendles what a pleasure."

"Jaxson Lyles, it's been a long time!" I stood and he grabbed me up in his arms and squeezed me tight. Hadn't felt this close and safe to a man in a while and even though me and Lake were done I still felt guilty because he didn't know that because he was still out. I slowly slithered my way from his grasp and he eventually released his hold.

"Damn Mira just as beautiful as I remember." He tucked his bottom lip between his teeth and glared at me. I couldn't deny the fact that I felt sexy under his stare. "So, where's that nigga you left me for?" The disdain in his voice for Lake was evident and I shook my head.

Jaxson and I were together when I met Lake. Jaxson was an amazing man, he was sweet and he had a good head on his shoulders. He wanted forever with me but I was young and hot in the ass, only thing on my mind was having fun and hanging out. Jaxson was going off to school and that wasn't on my agenda.

When I met Lake, he was charming and handsome, he didn't have a lot of money but he was a hustler and he knocked me off of my feet. I knew he was the one I wanted to be with so I ended up cheating on Jaxson. Guilty, I told him and he left me and went off to school. Last I heard he was some big shot marketing executive and engaged to be married.

"Lake is in the hospital in a coma right now." I said and he immediately regretted his prior statement. Even though he hated Lake for me, he knew that I loved him and he loved me enough to accept that.

"I'm so sorry Mira, what happened." Just that fast he was back to the caring Jaxson that I knew he could be.

"He got shot while he was at his side chick's, who turned out to be his wife's, house." I chuckled nervously. "Ironic huh? I cheated on you with him and he turns around and cheats on me and gets married." I shook my head. "I hate the day I met him."

"Don't you say that; don't you ever say that because if you hadn't met him you wouldn't have those beautiful twins." He smiled and I looked at him like he was crazy. "Don't look at me like that, just because you broke my heart don't mean that I didn't keep tabs on you." He inadvertently licked his lips. "You're always my favorite girl."

I smiled because he used to tell me all the time that no matter what we went through I was always his favorite girl. I could be literally screaming my head off at him and he would kiss me and say that I was his favorite girl.

"How's your fiancé, wife?" I probed.

"Oh, shit you been checking up on me too." He flapped his

jacket and then straightened it up like he was preparing for a picture. "That didn't work out." He didn't seem sad about it; his words were fluid and emotionless.

"Oh no why not, what happened?"

"You want the truth?" He raised a brow and slipped his hands in his pockets. I nodded my head, even though I had had enough *truth* to last a life time I still wanted to know his. "She wasn't you."

I cleared my throat and sat back down in the seat that I was previously occupying before he snatched me up. My eyes absorbed his caramel colored skin and the way his broad shoulders filled up the tailored suit that he wore. His light brown eyes bore into mine as he ran his tongue across his thick lips. His tall frame towered over me and it took me back to the days when things were good.

Jaxson always had a way of making you see things a certain way. Even now, he was right about the fact that Lake blessed me with my twins and I would forever be grateful but I wish I would have saved myself the heartache of dealing with him.

"Look Jaxson, I just got out of a shitty ass relationship. I mean shit that you would never think that I would allow myself to go through. My child's father is laying in a hospital bed and we don't know if he gone make it or not. Shit is just all fucked up right now. I'm in a vulnerable place and I don't want me to connect with you on no rev—"

"Stop right there, I don't want to hear the rest of what you have to say. We better than that. This shit right here was fate, you needed time to grow into the woman that you are today. You needed to go through the shit that you went through with Lake to prepare yourself to be with me." He smirked. "I prayed to God that he showed me who I was supposed to spend the rest of my life with and when I walked into this bar I knew right then who he was leading me to. I know you need time but I'm gone be there for you while you going through this, and you," he took his finger and lifted my chin so that I was looking directly into his eyes, "are going to let me."

With that he slid his card on the bar and patted it, leaned down and kissed my lips and then he was gone just as quickly as he came.

"I got too much on my plate right now to deal with entertaining another man." I sighed and tapped the card leaving it on the bar, I got up and headed to the door. When I got to the door I stopped and thought about my life and how everything lately has unfolded. I turned around and grabbed that card and slid it in my purse. I deserved to be happy too, I would just close one door before I opened another.

CHAPTER 9

$\mathcal{M}$*itch*

"You need to get on this and quick, I want him out of the way!" Chief Shriel screamed over the phone. "How in the fuck did he get those pictures? I do a lot for you to be safe out there. I shouldn't be going through this."

"I don't even know what the fuck you're going through, if anyone should be bitching it should be me. I pay you damn good money to make shit run smooth for me, so imagine my surprise when I put Heart's bitch ass away and then all of a sudden he's walking the streets." I yelled into the phone.

"I didn't have a choice! He had pictures of me, some of them more recent than I'm comfortable with. What was I supposed to do? Call his fucking bluff?"

"Heart doesn't operate like that, so someone else did that shit."

"You don't know that shit, and I'm not inclined to take the word of a half assed drug dealer that don't know how to control his people. Now fix this shit before I have to sever our ties because when it comes down to it I'll choose my career every time." He said all in one breath.

"Look I got shit under control, you don't worry about shit on my end. You do what the fuck I pay you to do." I hated when this white muthafucka tries to boss up. He didn't run shit and he knew it. He had as much leeway as I allowed him to have

"You better have shit under control, I would hate to let them know who really was behind the death of Big L." The blood in my veins froze at the thought of anyone finding out that I had something to do with Big L's death. I had forced myself to forget that day but here it was.

That shit was a power move and it worked and was the main reason I was in the position that I was in today. If I had to do that shit again I wouldn't hesitate. I just hate that this muthafucka held that card.

"I got this shit." I tried to sound confident but he had knocked me off my square with that shit.

"Yeah says the man that can't even control his fucking wife. Ask her where she was earlier." With hat he hung up and left me with my thoughts. Wynn was supposed to be visiting her father which I thought was strange in itself. Normally when Wyndel came into town he would call me. I picked up the phone and sent a call to my wife that went unanswered.

"Where the fuck is she? I don't have time for this."

Everything was starting to turn to shit. I shot Lake and that nigga didn't fucking die then Heart tried to kill my fucking ass and got out of jail without being processed. How in the hell did that shit happen? I had way too much clout for him to be moving like that. He had to have someone moving with him I just needed to find out who.

I wasn't in the mood to have to watch my back 24/7 but it looked like I didn't have a choice. I needed to holla at Mello, I called him and his phone went to voicemail too. What the fuck was going on?

I stood up and grabbed my keys, I was currently at the warehouse checking up on the numbers and handling business. Even though I got my shit from Wynn's dad, I had a few side deals on the back end that no one knew about, not even Mello.

Making sure that I had a backup plan is what kept me in the game for as long as I had been. Other people didn't believe in that shit, all they wanted to live off of was loyalty but that shit didn't pay my bills.

When I pulled up at the house both Wynn's car and Mello's car was in my drive way and that shit sent off alarms. What the fuck was Mello doing at my crib while I'm not there? We don't do that, never have never will.

Rushing up to the door when I opened it, Wynn and Mello was in the middle of a heated discussion. The minute they saw me they were both like deer caught in headlights.

"Hey baby." Wynn rushed over to me and threw her arms around my neck. "I've been waiting on you to get here."

"Oh yeah." I looked back and forth between the two of them. Mello seemed like he was upset about something and this nagging feeling in the pit of my gut was telling me that it had to do with my wife. "Where were you earlier?" I asked her with my eyes on Mello.

"Huh? Um, I was visiting my dad," her eyes nervously darted around the room. "I already told you that." She released her arms from around my neck and then took a step back. She glanced over at Mello who now had a smirk on his face.

"Yeah, so ya pops in the hospital and no one told me?" her body stiffened and that was the number one sign that she was lying, I had gotten the answer that I was looking for. Turning my attention to Mello who was now uncomfortable. "What you doing here?"

He released a heavy sigh and then looked at Wynn, who looked like she was about to shit herself at any moment. I took a step back from her and slipped my hands in my pockets. She had been on some bullshit for a while now and I was starting to think that Mello had something to do with that.

"Look Mitch, there's no easy way to tell you this I—"

"He came over here because I called him," Wynn hurriedly jumped in, she grabbed my arm and I jerked back. "I just found out that I was pregnant and I didn't know how to tell you. I didn't know how you would react so I called him," she blurted out in one breath.

I looked over at Mello and he had an uneasy look on his face that quickly washed over with anger. He was pissed and I wanted to know why.

"What's up Mello? Is that true? You look pressed over there." I cocked my head to the side and waited on his answer.

"Nah bruh we good. Yeah, she just didn't know how or if she wanted to tell you about *the baby*," the way he said *the baby* told a story that I didn't know if I wanted to read into. "But I'm out, holla at me if you need me." His statement wasn't towards me though.

We both watched as Mello left my house, after the door was shut and it was just us, we were surrounded by a thick layer of tension that made us both uncomfortable. Me because I didn't want to believe that my wife was stepping out on me with not only my best friend but my fucking enemy.

The way shit was starting to crumble around my ass this was the last thing that I needed. If I found out some shit was going down I promise on my life that I was killing both of them and I would deal with Wyndel later.

"I made reservations at our favorite restaurant." She said heading towards the stairs like nothing was wrong. I grabbed her arms and pulled her back to me. Looking down into her eyes I could see the deceit pouring out of them and I had to admit it hurt.

I know I did my thing but Wynn was always my constant, my backbone, my forever. I always knew that when all this drug shit was over and I was ready to settle down that I would have her and we would live happily ever after. My heart was telling me that it was all a dream and I was about to get one hell of a wakeup call.

"You love me, right?" I asked her and she searched my eyes for what I was thinking but I wouldn't let her in on that.

"Of course, I mean we have our shit but you know I love

you." She kissed me but I didn't return the gesture, I just nodded my head and let her arm go.

"What time are the reservations?" I asked.

"In an hour, I'm gonna go freshen up."

~

"Thank you for dining at Epic Steakhouse, name please?" the host looked up at us with the biggest smile on his face but my attention was somewhere else.

"Bings." Wynn proudly said, almost too proud, I tore my attention away from the sight before me and glared at her. She smiled and strutted her beautiful ass past me, following the host.

I diverted my attention back to the table that housed the sexy Mira and a man that I wasn't familiar with. I slipped my hands in my pockets and purposely walked past our table and walked by theirs. She was so enthralled in their conversation that she didn't even feel me standing there. I watched as she blushed and giggled like he was saying the funniest thing in the world. Her beautiful smile had me jealous as fuck at whoever this nigga was.

"Can we help you nigga?" the nigga she was eating with interrupted my nasty thoughts that were dancing around my mind. When I looked over at him he had a displeased look on his face but before I could address that Wynn walked over and joined us.

"Mitch do you know the—" Wynn's words were cut short by Mira throwing her drink in her face. She jumped up and went to swing but I grabbed her and pushed her back.

"Aye get your fucking hands off of her!" the nigga that she was with stood up jerked her back his way. "You good baby?" he asked as if he was familiar with her. I had just seen her a week or so ago and she was acting all stand offish like she was still stressing over that nigga.

"Yeah Jaxson I'm good but I owe that bitch!" she yelled pointing at Wynn who was standing there like a raging bull. "Why the fuck are you with her? Who is she?" She directed that question to me.

"I'm his fucking wife." Wynn answered for me with her hands on her hips. "Why the fuck do you care?"

"Well Mr. Mitch wasn't too married when he was trying to take my ass home with him just last week." She rolled her eyes at me. "And yo ass wasn't too married when I caught you riding my nigga Lake's dick in the car that's in my got damn name!" she yelled gaining the attention of everyone in the restaurant. "Don't look so caught up now, you lucky I can't get to you. You think I whooped yo ass the last time?" She pointed in Wynn's direction.

It was like something hit me and everything was coming together, shit was starting to make fucking sense. Lake didn't touch Wynn, she got her ass whooped because she was fucking that nigga. She the reason I got beef with these niggas. I looked over at her and she was looking at me with apologetic eyes but I didn't have not even an ounce of sympathy for her. It was fuck her right now.

"Mira let's go." The nigga Jaxson grabbed her hand and led her out the door. When they got to the door she turned to me and looked at me shaking her head.

"She was fucking him for months because I followed Lake to the apartment that she has in Stone Creek."

"What fucking apartment?" I yelled unintentionally and stepped towards her.

"She's lying!" Wynn yelled but her words lacked confidence.

"I bet you didn't know you was fucking with a married man," Mira smirked.

"You're fucking lying, that crazy bitch at the hospital said the same thing. If he was married I would know."

"Why the fuck do you care if he's married or not!" I yelled so loud it caused Wynn and the table sitting beside where she was standing to jump."

"Yeah bitch, I thought the same thing." She laughed and walked out of the restaurant with that nigga in tow.

Wynn's face was covered with embarrassment and guilt, I couldn't even handle her right now in fear that I would kill her. I would deal with her later. I turned and walked out of the restaurant leaving her standing there. I got in my car and left. Shit was going wrong on so many levels. I needed to get shit rolling and right now.

"Hello," Lil Jay answered on the first ring.

"Aye I need for you and Jason to handle some shit for me."

"You know we got you unc." He said knowing that he was dumb as hell and wouldn't have shit. He was bound to fuck some shit up but I had to let him prove himself.

"Meet me at the crib in 20."

"Say less."

CHAPTER 10

$\mathcal{L}$*ake*

I fucked up, I mean I royally fucked up. How in the fuck was I gone fix this shit? I never in a million years would have thought that Miracle would out ya boy. She apologizes every day for telling Mira about us but that apology wasn't going to mend the issue that she caused. I knew what I did was fucked up but I wanted to tell Mira in my own way and on my own time, preferably when I was divorced and after I married her.

I don't know if it was gonna be possible to get Mira back after this and I didn't know if I could live without her. I needed her in my life, I needed my kids in my life. Fuck! I needed to get my eyes open so that I could try my best to salvage this shit.

"Baby I need you to wake up, me and this baby need you." I could hear Miracle crying.

She had been here faithfully every time I tried to wake up, she's the first person I hear. Only problem with that was, her voice wasn't the one I wanted to hear. Where the fuck was Mira?

Love wasn't what I would describe as the foundation of me and Miracle. I got love for shorty but not in the way that I wanted to spend the rest of my life with her. She was young and did whatever I asked of her. She was my little rider and it didn't take much to please her.

Don't get me wrong shorty got a strong head on her shoulders and she's a go getter and got plans to make something of herself. Hell, if I hadn't of fell for Mira so hard then Miracle would definitely be what she was trying so desperately to be. I just never opened myself up to her the way I had to Mira, Miracle got what I allowed for her to get.

This shit sounded fucked up but when it came down to it, that's just the way shit was. I got to get the fuck up out of here. Heart came to see me and told me that he was out there looking for Mitch and I didn't want him doing that shit himself.

Last night when he came by he said that he had been watching Mitch and was just waiting on the right time to get at him. He's also been checking for his hoe ass wife just in case and she been moving foul too. I wanted him to wait on me, I wanted to handle this shit myself.

Get the fuck up Lake!

Get the fuck up and handle yo fucking business nigga! I coached myself as I slowly opened my eyes and was met with a bright light. I hurriedly shut them and let my eyes readjust and then opened them again.

Miracle had her head down in my lap with her face turned away from me, she was woke because I could hear her sniffing. I couldn't talk because there was something down my throat so I tried to move my hand, it was heavy as fuck but I was able to touch her head.

"Ahhh oh my god! You're awake! Oh, thank you Jesus!" she cried out with a fresh stream of tears flowing down her face. "Thank God, baby I'm glad you're back!"

I nodded my head and then pointed at my mouth, she looked at what I was pointing at and ran and got the doctor. They all rushed in the room and began to work on me and ran a bunch of test but they never took the shit out of my mouth so I went to grab it.

"Hold on Mr. Childs, we just need to make sure it's okay to take that out," he tried to tell me but I pointed at it a final time. The doctor nodded his head and got the nurse to help him take it out. When that shit came out there was green shit that came with it. I tried to talk and ask what the fuck it was but my shit was raw as fuck. "Don't try and speak right now, let's get you to take a few sips of water." The doctor advised as the nurse brought over a cup of water.

"Slow sips okay." When she put the straw in my mouth I gulped down that water so fast and it felt like my throat was on fire. I winced at the pain and I could have sworn I saw that nurse laugh.

"Fuck!" my voice was low and raspy but it was there and that's all that matters. The doctor gave instructions on what to and not to do while I'm trying to recover. I wasn't listening to anything they were saying, I was paying attention to my phone that was on the table next to me. I just needed to get it so I could text Mira.

About an hour later they were cleaning up and walking out of the room. Miracle sat over in the corner smiling like she had just won the lottery. I was appreciative for her being here with me but I wanted to see my kids and Mira.

"How you feeling?" she asked walking over to me. "Oh, shit I forgot, the doctor don't want you to talk a lot." She smiled as she rubbed my head. I tried to sit up but a pain shot through my side and I almost cried. "Sit still you're gonna hurt yourself."

"I'M GOOD!" I yelled out unintentionally causing her to jump back. I could see the tears pool in her eyes as she walked over to the windowsill and sat on it bringing her knees to her chest. "Look I'm sorry I just—"

"Nah don't apologize." She didn't even look my way, she pulled out her phone and dialed a number. "Hey La, no everything is okay. I just wanted to let you and Heart know that he's up." Her tone was sad and defeated. "They're on their way."

"Miracle come here." I said to her and she shook her head. She was being extremely emotional and I had never known her to be like that. She was a rowdy chick with a slick mouth, normally she would have cussed my ass out. This baby had her on some other shit. "Please!"

After a few moment she wiped her face with the back of her hands and slid down out of the windowsill. When she stood up she stretched and her perfect perky breast sat up nice in the tight V-neck shirt she had on. I could see her dime sized nipples poking through the thin fabric, for the first time in a while I felt my man rise.

That was one thing that we did have, a sexual connection. I don't think there was a woman out there who could please me like Miracle could, not even Mira. No matter how much I tried to say that Mira was the best I ever had, Miracle puts her to sleep in the bedroom. Too bad my heart didn't live there.

"Yes!" she said as she got over to me. Her smooth vanilla skin had a beautiful glow to it, her lips were formed in a frown making her puffy eyes more obvious to the fact that she had been crying. Her hips had spread a little and her stomach wasn't washboard flat like it was before.

"How long have I been in here?" I looked around the room.

"Almost a month."

"A fucking month? You've been here a month?" she nodded her head, I ran my hand down my face and had to wince at the pain. "Fuck."

"You need to be careful."

Pulling the covers back, I looked at the damage that was done and got pissed all over again as my mind flashed back to me walking out of the building. I couldn't wait to get my hands on that nigga.

"Tell me what happened?" I looked at her. "What happened that made you *have to* tell our secret?"

I couldn't quite read the look on her face, it was somewhere between pissed off and *you can't be fucking serious*. "She told me that I didn't have a right to be there and she was about to try and have me put out the hospital. I wasn't having that and she wasn't about to sit there and make life decisions for my husband, point, blank, period." She said with finality. "I'm so over everybody treating me like I'm the fucking bad guy, everybody running around acting like they got to protect poor Mira. No fuck that, what the fuck about me? I'm the one sitting here pregnant by my fucking husband and taking shots for it like what the fuck? What about my got damn feelings?" She yelled my way.

I was almost scared to say anything else, the look in her eyes warned me not to. I nodded my head. She stood there and shook her head with tears streaming down her face. It made a nigga feel like shit. Miracle was a damn good woman she's just not the woman I wanted to build a life with.

"Aye look—" I started but was cut off by the door swinging open.

"My muthafuckin nigga!" Heart said as he walked over to the bed and pulled me into a hug. The shit hurt like a muthafucka but I could tell that his ass had been through it since I was out so I didn't say shit. He also had death in his eyes so I knew that shit was coming and soon. "Got damn you scared a nigga." He finally released me.

"Man, hell I scared myself, I thought that was it for ya boy." I said truthfully. The tension in the room was thick as fuck, everybody seemed uncomfortable to be in each other's presence and that was weird because we were all cool as fuck.

"I'll come back later." Miracle said with defeat evident in her voice. I gave her a sympathetic look, even though I hated that I was hurting her like I was. She didn't bother to speak or say much to Heart or Lala and I had a good notion that it had to do with the *secret.*

Lala glance at Miracle's back as she walked out but she never said anything, once she was gone she released a heavy sigh. I hoped like hell they weren't beefing because of me. When she turned back towards me tears were pooling her eyes.

"Are you going to be okay?" She asked crossing her arms across her chest.

"Yeah they said with a little bit of time and some kind of therapy to strengthen my core I'mma be straight." I laid back and winced as my torso stretched back out.

"Good!" she said but I knew that wasn't the last of what she had to say. "How in the fuck could you do that to Mira, Lake? She's been nothing but good to you. She's been there for you through all this shit and you go and get married and to Miracle of all people! What the fuck were you thinking?"

"Shit ain't what you think it is."

"Nah fuck all that shit, I heard about the bullshit reason that you married her Lake but she seems to think that you love her and after this it's gonna be you and her till the end of fucking time." She was so pissed spit was flying from her mouth but it never delayed her from telling me everything she thought about the situation. "What were you thinking? You know she would have never turned on you Lake, you knew she wouldn't have ratted you out. She ain't built like that and you know it so be real with us."

"Lala, I didn't know that shit! She was a young ass girl that watched me cap a nigga."

"That was trying to get at her! You gotta do better than that Lake I ain't buying that shit and I'm younger than she is." She popped her hip out. Lala has always had attitude on her but I just wasn't used to being on the receiving end of it.

"You don't know that and neither did I, and to be honest I wasn't about to bank my fucking life on it. Who's to say she didn't get pissed because I wouldn't fucking leave Mira and decide to hold that shit over my head? Nah fuck that I did what the fuck I had to do and when I talk to Mira I'll let her know that."

People may not understand why I did what I did, but in my eyes, it was the only fucking choice so I did that shit. Miracle *loved* me so much that when I told her we could get married as long as she gave me time to set shit right with Mira and so long as she didn't tell anyone about it she agreed.

I always knew that it wouldn't last long enough for Mira to find out but then after time she started showing her loyalty to me and she became someone that I looked forward to seeing. She became my peace and the marriage wasn't hurting no one so I didn't stress it.

Of course, I would have to get the divorce when it was time to marry Mira but I planned on dealing with that shit when the time came. Me and Mira had some shit to work out before we actually were ready to take that step, I had time to figure shit out or so I thought.

"Yo ass done caused a fucking shit storm my nigga and I need you to figure that shit out before it's too late." Heart gave me a look that said it wasn't a request. He was telling me to fix the shit or we would have problems and the last thing that I needed right now was issues with my brother. "We got too much going on for Mira and Miracle to be fighting and stalking each other and shit," he chuckled but it wasn't in a joking way, it was more him thinking about the reality of the situation.

I had caused a beef between two strong minded females who both loved me equally. I ran my hands down my face and sighed heavily. Some shit was about to go down and I wasn't ready for it.

"I'm gonna go check on Mira." Lala said with a roll of the eyes.

"You always rolling yo damn eyes." I picked with her.

"Well when you around ignorant bullshit you ain't got a choice." She shrugged her shoulder. I could see the disappointment in her eyes. As much as I wanted to tell her that I would make shit right I didn't know that to be true so I kept that shit to myself.

"Aye wait for me, you don't need to be out by yourself with that bitch Mitch still breathing."

"We need to take care of that shit and asap!"

"Yeah, I agree but right now I'm moving smart, they already got me for fucking his ass up so if that nigga come up missing they gone be looking at my ass. So, for now as long as I got eyes on him I know La safe and that's what I'm focused on right now."

"How in the fuck did you get out of that shit anyway? When I was out I could hear you talking about it La. I could hear every damn thing I just couldn't wake the fuck up."

"So, you heard me call you a dumb ass whack ass coward son of a bitch?" La smirked still holding on to the door knob.

"I heard all that shit nigga." I grilled her and for the first time since she walked in the room she smiled and it felt good to see that there was still some kind of love there. "But what's up, who the fuck you snitch on? You got out that bitch fast."

"Fuck you nigga, I ain't no fucking snitch." He flipped me off. "But to be honest I don't even know. La said she called Darren, the nigga that used to run with Big L," he waited for me to let him know that I knew who he was referring to.

"Yeah I knew D man, that nigga used to get us out of trouble all the fucking time." We both laughed thinking back to all the shit we used to be on.

"Well he still doing that shit, cause I just knew my ass was about to dress the fuck out but they had me sitting in that holding cell forever then all of a sudden some bitch ass CO came and took me to the Chief of Police Shriel or some shit like that. He started talking about some fucking pictures and how much to make that shit go away. I told his ass I didn't know what the fuck he was talking about and his bitch ass tried to threaten me but you know how that go." Heart smiled and crossed his arms across his chest.

"We need to holla at that nigga."

"Yeah but another day, you need to rest so you can get the fuck out of here and we can handle this fucking business. I'm tired of this nigga breathing, taking up all my air and shit."

"Hopefully I can get the fuck out of here soon, they bringing in a physical therapist tomorrow to see if I can walk and shit. I told them I can, only thing wrong with me is this big ass hole in my fucking chest." I grabbed my chest for emphasis. "Once that shit stop being fucking sore I'll be back to terrorizing the fucking streets."

"And people's hearts." Lala said sadly. "I'm gonna be outside, I'm gonna try and call Mira again." Heart nodded his head and watched Lala walk out of the door.

"Nigga this shit fucked up, she ain't even talking to Miracle right now and they need each other. I feel bad as fuck for Miracle cause everybody turned their backs on her. She didn't give a fuck though, she was right here with you not giving a fuck."

"I know, and I feel bad as shit for what I'm about to do to her." Heart gave me a look that I couldn't quite interpret, he didn't say shit he just turned and left.

No one understood the shit that I was in and I didn't expect them to. When it came down to it was my life and my decision, that was already made.

CHAPTER 11

*L*ala

    I don't know what the fuck is wrong with Mira, I have been calling her and calling her to let her know that Lake was up but she wasn't answering. A part of me was worried and the other part felt like she had crawled back in her stubborn hole.

This month that Lake had been down has been hell on all of us but mostly her because she needed answers and he was the only person that could give them to her. She was so confused and heartbroken that she shut everybody out.

I was surprised when she called me and asked me to watch the kids last week because her mom went and visited family in Florida and she had something to do. I didn't hesitate. I had her bring them to the house and me and Heart took them out to the trampoline park and for ice cream.

Since then she went right back into her not texting or answering phone calls and the shit had me feeling a kind of way. She told me out of her own mouth that she didn't believe that I knew anything about the relationship or the marriage, yet she's still pushing me away. Friends don't do that shit.

If you hurting sis lets hurt together, that's how I always seen it but everyone ain't built like me. We pulled up to her house and her car was there, the sun was just going down but her blinds were already closed which led me to believe that she wasn't there.

"Where is she?" I said more to myself than anyone else.

"Babe we did just pop up," Heart said from the car, I was currently walking away from the door that I had just knocked on.

"Well she ain't answering calls and she needs to know that Lake is up because they need to talk."

"Lala don't push, you thinking that the talking is gone solve all of their issues. You're hoping that the conversation is gone give them something that they don't already have. I get that you want everything to be okay but it ain't that simple. A lot of shit been done. Just let shit happen."

"I mean if anything the kids need to see him." I ignored what he said because a part of it was true. Somewhere in the back of my mind I was hoping that after a conversation everything would just go back to the way it was before everything came crumbling down.

My attention was stolen away by a gunmetal BMW 750i with tinted windows. That car was nice and smooth, looked like it should belong to an older gentleman. When the door opened and this tall fine ass caramel skin nigga stepped out of the car I almost drooled.

"Lala don't get fucked up." Heart yelled getting out of the car. I snapped my head back and reached out for Heart. The nigga was fine but he was no match for my nigga. "Who the fuck is that and why the fuck is he here at my nigga house?"

Heart said that shit loud enough for the whole neighborhood to hear it, and when the dude stopped walking in mid stride I knew that he heard it to. I could see the corners of his mouth turn up into a smirk but he didn't say anything. *Damn and he's cocky too.* I thought to myself.

"I see you haven't changed one-bit Heart." He finally uttered a word as he leaned down and opened the door, when Mira stepped out of the car dressed to kill I wanted to do just that, kill her.

"Mira what the fuck are you doing and who the fuck is this?"

"Jaxson?" Heart said squinting his eyes to get a better look.

"You know him?" I asked Heart who now wore a scowl, he was shaking his head like he knew something that I didn't.

"Yeah that's the nigga Lake stole Mira from." Heart threw out with malice in his voice. "The fuck you doing Jaxson?" Heart took a few steps toward him but I put my hands up to stop him. He glared at the Jaxson dude but he never waivered, he didn't seem phased by the distain in Heart's demeanor, if you asked me he was inviting it.

I didn't know what history the two of them had but it was weird. It was like there was some kind of unspoken line of respect that was being tampered with and Heart was feeling it. Jaxson turned to us once he had Mira safely out of the car.

"Look Heart, you know we ain't got no beef. You like my got damn brother but Mira said she was single and I wasn't gone miss out on my forever because of some bullshit ass agreement we had years ago."

"What are you talking about? What agreement?" Mira asked looking back and forth between the two of them. That was the first time she's spoke up since they got here. My blood was starting to boil but I kept my mouth shut.

"After you cheated on me with Lake," Jaxson started and looked down at Mira who lowered her head. "I was pissed, I hated you so when this nigga offered me money to bounce that's what I did. We all used to run money for Big L but I had a scholarship to go to school and I was taking that shit, but when you cheated I felt like you had made your decision. So, it was a win, win for me. The nigga said to stay away from you and I did. Next thing I hear you pregnant and living the good life and I was off in school so I figured I made the right decision."

"Wow it was that easy for you to give up on me?" she looked up at his tall frame.

"Was it that easy for you to give up on me?" he countered her.

"We'll talk about this later." She warned him.

"Oh, we will." He said not backing down.

"What are y'all doing here, what is it now?"

"Lake is woke." I simply said and that shit took the attitude out of her. Her eyes watered over and her lip started to tremble. Jaxson looked down at her and she straightened her face.

"Well the kids are with my mom and they'll be back next week, I'll bring them up to see him then. No need in me going if the kids aren't here."

"Mira, I know you hurting but be smart about this. Just a little while ago you were talking about how hurt you were that Lake got married on you and how much you loved him and now you shacking up with your ex in a house that Lake bought you." I snarled my nose up, I couldn't hide the distaste that I had for the women in my circle right now. "Don't go opening up a bunch of doors until you figure out if the one you and Lake's family lives behind is closed and locked."

"That door was closed and locked the minute your little bitch ass friend stated that her name was Miracle Childs." She rolled her neck.

"Yo that was some fucked up shit but damn give the nigga a chance to explain what the fuck was going on. It's more than what you think it is." Heart tried to reason with her but she wasn't trying to hear it. She waved him off and placed her hands on her hips.

"I really can't believe you two, out of all people y'all know better than anyone the shit that I've done and sacrificed for this man and to be handled like I'm some kind of side chick, ha!" she released a frustrated laugh. "See where you got it wrong is I don't owe Lake a got damn thing but he on the other hand owes me an explanation of what the hell happened and I plan on cashing in on that but I can promise you that it won't change anything. I'm done, I refused to be that girl."

"It's not about being that girl Mira, fuck all that bullshit and what other people think. This about your family and if you're willing to save it."

"Lala, I love you girl but your *everything in the world will be alright* attitude is making me fucking sick. Mind your business and focus on your relationship with Heart, you two are good for each other, y'all got something real. Just don't let anything or anyone come in and ruin that, promise me."

The lone tear that rolled down her eyes made my heart hurt for her. "Just slow down Mira, you've got kids to think about." She laughed at what I said before she took Jaxon's hands and led him to the front door.

Before she opened the door, she turned and looked at me, "Everything happens for a reason and even though y'all may want things between me and Lake to work they won't. I'll never trust that man another day of my life and who wants to live like that?" she shrugged. "If I'm not happy my kids can't be happy so let me be," she looked at Jaxson and then back at me, "happy."

The smile that she delivered to me caused tears to roll down my face. A huge part of me felt like she was using this Jaxson guy to get rid of the feelings that she knew were there for Lake. He was her rebound guy, I just had a feeling that it was gonna blow up in her face. I just hoped I was wrong.

"Let's go La," Heart was pissed and I could hear it in his tone but I wasn't gone speak on it and I knew that he was going to tell

Lake what just happened and to be honest he had a right to know. He couldn't really be mad because he put this shit on himself.

I on the other hand, was conflicted. A part of me felt like Mira deserved to be happy and on her terms but the other part of me feels like she should try and fight for her family. I didn't know how I would feel about all of this if I were in her shoes so I was trying to chill out with judging her moves. I just hoped like hell that she was smart about her decisions, for her and her kid's sake.

CHAPTER 12

M *ira*

"Thank you so much for being there for me just now, that was a lot." I said laying my pocketbook on the kitchen table. "And sorry I made them think that we were more than just friends." I don't even know why I did that, it wasn't like it mattered but for some reason I felt the need for them to think that he was my man. In some way I felt like that hurt would get back to Lake.

I had my back turned towards him and he walked up behind me and enclosed me in his arms. I could feel his semi hard dick pressing against my ass. I unintentionally moaned in his embrace as I collapsed in his arms.

"You don't have to apologize, I told you that I was here for you no strings attached. Plus, for a minute there I enjoyed the thought of being the man that was making you happy." He chuckled. "But I know that's not what you need right now. Right now, you need a friend who's gone be there for you and keep it real with you."

He let me go and turned me around to face him. The sympathy in his eyes was enough for me to drop my panties and ride his face but like he said, that's not what I needed. He rubbed his hands up and down my arms making me forget about everything that I just thought.

"I want you to make love to me." I said against my better judgement. "No talking, no telling me what I need to do. I just want you to pin my legs behind my head and fuck every ounce of heartache, pain and sorrow out of me. As my friend that's what I need." I glanced into his honey colored eyes and got lost in his story.

From that day in the bar we've been spending so much time together. My mom went to visit her family and when she came back she said that she wanted to take the kids. They've been gone for a week and due to come back next week so it has given me time to reconnect with Jaxson.

He's been nothing but the perfect gentlemen and a great friend. He keeps it real with me and hasn't tried to fuck me once. If it weren't for him I would have never been able to get to a point where I can think about the situation without crying or spazzing.

I've been up to the hospital a few times and every time I go *she's* there and I refused to sit up there with her like we sister wives or some shit so I stopped going. I figured I'd wait until someone comes and tells me that he's awake.

"Earth to Mira." When I snapped out of my thoughts Jaxson was waving his hands in my face trying to get my attention. "Where'd you go?"

"Just thinking about everything, I'm sorry."

"Stop saying that, stop apologizing. You've been through some straight up bullshit in the last month and I get it. But you have to stop thinking with your emotions. Sex right now would be great," he smirked and bit his bottom lip, "we both know that but it wouldn't be smart. Like your friend Lala said, you need to close all doors before you open up another one. I'd give anything to show you what I have to offer, physically, mentally and spiritually but not until I know you're ready." He grabbed my face and stared into my eyes. "Right now, you are not ready."

"Did you mean what you said out there, about missing out on your forever?" A part of me felt like he was just playing the part that I needed him to play but something about the way he said it made it feel real and I wanted to know if it was real or not.

"I meant every word, I believe that it was meant for me to walk into that bar that night. I wasn't even coming this way that night, I was supposed to be headed to Statesville but something pulled me in that direction and I believe that it was your spirit. I'm not like most men, I'm not gone just fuck you because I know you're in a bad place, I can't do that. It also doesn't mean that I'm going to find solace in another woman while I'm being there for you. Take your time to figure shit out and I'll just be here making sure we're on the same page. As for forever, the second you feel like you're ready we'll start the clock on that," he smiled and my knees gave out, he had to catch me.

"Why didn't I choose you?" I don't know where all of these emotions came from but the tears started to flow and I couldn't stop them. I was hurt and tired of feeling the way I was feeling over Lake.

"Like I said everything happens for a reason." He held me in his arms while I cried. "Now what I'm about to say to you may piss you off but you need to hear it."

"No lectures." He's been telling me that I needed to stop running off of emotions since the night we talked at the bar. He always knew what to say and do to make a fucked-up situation better. I needed to keep him around one way or the other.

"You need to go and see him, you need to find out if what happened is enough to say fuck y'all." I tried to move from his embrace but he pulled me back. "You can't live with all of this unanswered and plan to be happy. It's not possible, you're going to always have that shit in the back of your mind and down the line it's gonna fuck with whatever you got going." He enclosed me in this arms again and rested his chin on my head. "You gotta close that door before you open ours."

I sighed heavily, there was nothing else to be said. He was right and I deserved the answers to the questions that were in my heart.

"*M*ira, baby!" was the first thing out of Lake's mouth when I walked in the hospital room. The way he called me baby turned my stomach. I didn't want him to refer to me in any way that would indicate that we were more than co parents. "A nigga happy you here, what took you so long to come? I know Lala told you what was up."

I scoffed at the audacity in his tone as if I owed him something. I had to take a few deep breaths to keep from blowing my shit because I knew that would help anything. I needed to have a level head about this, there were children involved.

"Lake the way I look at it, I don't owe you shit. I'm here as a courtesy for your kids."

"I know shit is all crazy right now but Mira I promise you that it's not what you think. I love you baby and I would never just hurt you like that if I had a choice. You got to believe me, the shit was life or death."

I walked closer to the bed and slapped the shit out of him. I could tell that I shocked him because his eyes stretched the size of saucers and his mouth was hanging open. I didn't know who he thought I was. I never showed him any reasons to think that I was a dumb bitch by any means so I was confused as to why he was treating me like one.

"Lake Childs, if no one else knows you I do and I know when you feeding me bullshit." I shook my head and he opened his mouth to speak but I held my hand up to stop him. "Do you know how hurt and humiliated I was when that bitch whipped out a marriage license? I don't think I had ever felt a pain like the one I felt in that moment. After everything that I had been to you and for you and that's the thanks I get? THAT YOU'RE FUCKING MARRIED!" I screamed.

"Mira, I'm sorry and you right, I couldn't imagine what the fuck you was feeling but I promise you on my kids that I'm gone fix this shit. You won't ever have to worry about me on that bull-shit again. It's just me and you from here on out."

I released a laugh that was on the verge of demented, "You think you have a choice in my future?" I shook my head. "You know there was a time that I *knew* without a shadow of a doubt that I was gone spend the rest of my life with you, that we would get married and have two more kids, another girl and boy." I smiled at the thought. "But you know what they say, if you want to make God laugh then tell him what you got planned." I laughed again but this time it was filled with the hurt I was feeling right now thinking about everything that we had been going through.

"Mira let me fix this, for our kids."

"Fix what? There is nothing to fix, I will never trust you again. You're fucking married Lake, MARRIED and not only that you fucking bitches in the car that your kids ride in, a car that I ride in Lake." I raised my voice a few octaves.

I pinched the bridge of my nose to calm myself down. I wasn't expecting to be this emotional. Jaxson was right, getting over this wasn't gone be easy by a long shot. Lake was going to always have a place in my heart because of where he took me emotionally but that's where it ends for me.

"Listen I had to get married to save my life, I—" he started but I cut him off again.

"I love you with everything in me Lake,"

"Mira, I love you too I just—" I cut him off again.

"I never knew just how much I loved you until just now, in this moment when I realized it wasn't enough. There isn't one thing that I would have or could have done different to make you be as loyal to me as I was to you and I'm okay with that. I'm at peace with it, that fact alone will help me grow from this situation."

"You are enough, my family is enough."

"Lake if we were I wouldn't be standing here forcing myself not to whoop yo ass."

"Mira, I love you like I've never loved anyone or anything else. I can't see myself without you."

"You should have thought about that before you went handing out last names and shit."

"She may have my last name but Mira you have my heart."

All of the tears that I had been holding at bay rolled down my face so fast I couldn't keep up with them, the more I wiped the more came down. As bad as I wanted to just forgive him and believe what he was saying about it all being a mistake I couldn't. If I forgave him this time it would just be a window for him to continue to treat me like this.

Plus, she is pregnant and I wasn't about to deal with no baby momma/wife drama. They could have that. I just wanted to raise my kids and be happy. Even though this made me realize that what Jaxson had been saying was true. I was looking forward to him being there with me through this process.

"The fucked-up part about it is I should have both." I said barely above a whisper.

"Mira please, just listen to me. Miracle saw me kill someone, I didn't know how loyal she was so I married her so she couldn't testify against me if it came back to me."

"Lake do you expect me to believe that shit? I don't even know that girl and I can tell that she loves the fuck out of you and would do anything you tell her to do. She's young and dumb and you had her wrapped around your finger. She would have took that secret to the grave. You didn't have to marry her, that's something you wanted to do." I shook my head.

"Y'all don't know what that girl would do. Miracle ain't as naïve as y'all may think, she's smart as fuck so I had to make sure that I was good. I knew I needed to be there for y'all, you and the kids."

"So, is that why you were fucking her too?" I raised an eyebrow and he opened his mouth to speak but he closed it back. He knew what he was saying was bullshit and so did I. "Exactly, that girl had all the confidence in the world when we first came up to the hospital. Like if I didn't live with you, sleep with you every night and have your kids I would have believed that she was the one that was with you for over 7 years." I had to chuckle at the thought.

"Miracle is like my best friend, I can talk to her about anything and she's there for me."

"Well if you feel like that and I wasn't there for you then

leave me alone, let me be happy and go on about my life. You don't love me like you say you do. I was comfortable for you, so I'm asking you to let me go."

"I can't do that."

"You don't have a choice Lake." I shook my head, right as I was about to leave the nurse walked in and looked around.

"I could have sworn I saw Mrs. Childs standing here just a minute ago." She looked from me to Lake. "I have some forms for her, if you see her tell her to stop by the front desk." Again, she looked at me and then Lake.

"I can sign them." He butted in looking at me. I could feel the warm tears touching my cheeks.

"I need her signature for these, just saying that she gave us permission for certain things. I was supposed to get those to her a while ago but the doctor took her verbal word for it so just have her come see me." she smiled and headed out the door.

"I'm sorry about that I—"

"Just save it Lake, just move on with your wife and new baby. We can co-parent."

"You think I'm about to let that shit happen?"

"Lake you don't really have a choice." I backed to the door, staring at him the entire time. Once I reached the door I spoke again, "You may wanna have a conversation with your wife about what she may have heard." With that I walked out and headed out the hospital.

When I got to the car I broke down. I cried like I've never cried in my life. I couldn't control the sobs, I was shaking I was so upset. Picking up my phone I dialed Jaxson.

"I—I—I ne—need you!" I barely got out.

"I'm on my way."

I waited until I got myself together and was calm enough to drive. I crunk the car and took off in the direction of my house. My heart was heavy and I didn't know if I could deal with this alone.

CHAPTER 13

*H*eart

"Shit!" I hissed as I worked my way in and out of Lala. I swear it was like I couldn't control myself when I was inside her. Neither one of us needed a kid right now but the last thing that I was gonna do is put on a rubber and I didn't have enough control to pull out. We were walking on a very thin line but we would just have to cross that bridge when we get there.

"Baby, you're gonna make me cum." She said grabbing my neck bringing my face to hers. When I was close enough for her lips to touch mine, she sucked in my bottom one causing my dick to twitch. "God, I love you."

"I love you! If you don't quit that shit though I'mma fill yo ass up." I said staring her in the eyes. Without saying anything else she began to move her hips in a circular motion under me making it hard for me to refrain from giving her the hard-long strokes that she was begging me for.

Leaning up so that I had more control I spread her legs by her thighs and put pressure on them so that I had the perfect view of her perfect pussy. Her clit was waving at me, I knew right then she was about to release.

I ground into her sex as far as I could and I let myself linger there, this was home and it felt hella good to be able to call it that. Since the day we made it official I hadn't thought about another woman not that I thought that would be a problem but it made me realize that this was real and the right move for me.

Pulling out, I slammed back into her making her raise up off the bed a little with her mouth hanging open. My thumb found her clit and I applied pressure as I delivered slow purposeful strokes.

"O—mah—gawd!" she yelled out. Her breathing started to pick up and her stomach got tight, she squeezed her eyes tight and when her legs began to tremble I continued my strokes until I felt the warm release of her pleasure rain down on my shaft. "Yesss yesss yesss oh god yes baby," she moaned and then she began to mumble something. I continued to give her slow strokes until her breathing calmed down a little.

"Come ride La."

"Ummmm I can't move my legs."

"Come ride or I'll make you regret saying no."

"Heart that's not fair." She whined as I pulled out of her watching her gasp made me bite my lip. Lala was so sexy from her pouty lips to her wide hips. Everything about her was perfect and right now all I wanted to do was to watch her breast bounce up and down while my dick disappears in her pussy.

I rolled over on my back but she had yet to move, her legs were still spread wide open and she was just lying there with her eyes closed. I don't know why she liked to test me but I was about to show her why she shouldn't.

Latching on to one of her dime sized nipples I ran my hand down the length of her stomach. When I reached her pussy, her eyes popped open but it was too late. I already had her clit between my thumb and index finger rolling it lightly, she loved when I did that shit except for when she was sensitive.

"Baby!"

"I told yo ass to get up and come ride, didn't I?" I said tucking my bottom lip between my teeth. "You didn't listen and now you gotta pay.

Jumping up I lowered myself so that I was eye level with her pussy. I glanced up at her and she was pleading with me to please her like only I could but her head was moving side to side like she was saying no. I've always been told that they eyes never lie so I covered her pussy with my mouth and began to suck.

Immediately I could taste the sweetness of her love and I went crazy from there. I sucked, licked and nibbled until she was pushing my head down to her and screaming my name.

"Fuck baby, shit right there."

"You gone ride this dick like I said?" I said against her pussy.

"Yes baby, I'm gonna do what you said, oh god yes." She yelled out as she tried to push my head further into her.

"What did I say?"

"Ummm shit I'm about to cum!"

"What did I say?" The vibrations of my voice against her clit had her going crazy. "I can't fucking hear you La."

"I'm gonna ride oh shit, I'm gonna, fuck I'm coming!" Her legs shook violently and she filled my mouth up with her sweet nectar. "Fuck yes, I wanna ride." She said out of breath.

I smirked and wiped the remainder of her juices off of my face with my hand. I laid back down and my dick stood straight up. It was something about pleasing her that turned me the fuck on. The shit never failed.

"Ummm my turn." La said as she crawled over to me and licked the head of my dick. I went to grab her to bring her to me but she slapped my hands away and drug her tongue around the head of my dick and then up and down the shaft.

"Don't fucking play with it." I taunted and she looked up at me with a smirk before she took all of me in her mouth and sucked as she bobbed her head up and down my shaft. "Oh fuck!"

"Umhmmmm!" she said with my dick still in her mouth. She went to work on my shit and baby girl wasn't letting up. The warm feel of her tongue sweeping the base of my dick while the head touched the back of her throat.

"Fuck La you gone make me nut!" I hissed. I was trying to hold back but I couldn't. Before I could stop myself, I was shooting a fresh load down her throat and she didn't even let up. She sucked harder until I couldn't even find the words to tell her to stop.

Once she felt like she had tortured me enough she popped my

dick out of her mouth and then licked her lips. I mugged her and she laughed. Without waiting on me to say anything she straddled me and eased down on my shit. A nigga was still sensitive so my eyes rolled to the back of my head involuntarily.

"This feels so good baby," she said as she rocked back and forth with her hands on my chest. "Gah you make me feel so good."

"That's what I'm supposed to do." I grabbed her waist to slow her down, I wanted to savor this shit but she was in control and she didn't have a problem showing me just that. She knew what her bouncing on my dick does to me. "Don't you even think about it La!" I warned her but the smile that spread across my face let me know I was fighting a losing battle.

Knock! Knock! Knock! Lala paused and looked at me like I was crazy. Who the fuck would be coming to Lala's house this time of night? It was after midnight.

"Who the fuck could that be?" Lala asked as I picked her up and sat her next to me.

"I don't know, but I'll be back." I looked at her and she had a look on her face that said fuck you. "Man just stay right here let me see who this is aight?" I asked her and she nodded her head. I knew she wasn't gone listen so I hoped this was Mira or somebody.

I went to the dresser and grabbed my gun just as the knocking stopped. I looked back at Lala and she shrugged her shoulders and grabbed her phone.

"No one had called." She laid the phone down and then reached in the nightstand pulling out a chromed-out baby 380.

"What the fuck you gone do with that?" I held up my nine to her 380.

"What the fuck I gotta do." She smirked. *Knock Knock Knock!*

I walked out of the room ass naked and stalked to the door, I looked through the peephole. What the fuck were they doing here? *Knock Knock!* I walked back to the room and slipped on the pair of shorts that I had on and instructed Lala to get dressed

By the time I got back to the door the knocking had stopped and I opened up the door. No one was there, I walked out of the apartment and saw Cynt and Darren about to leave.

"Aye!" I called out and they looked up at me.

"We thought y'all weren't home."

"Nah we here we were just busy." I said nonchalantly, I'm sure they knew what I meant but I didn't really care if they did or didn't.

I walked back in the house and headed to the bathroom so I could clean up a little bit. Lala was already in there. The door was unlocked just in case they decided to come back up. I heard the door open and shut, I knew it was them.

"Who is that?" La asked me and I looked at her trying to brace myself for what her reaction might be.

"Your mom and Darren." I said and then waited to see how she wanted to proceed forward. "If you want them to leave, I can make that happen. All you got to do is say the word."

She sighed heavily, "No I need to talk to them, I've made it my business to stay away from them. The last time I seen them was when I asked for help to get you out of jail. After then I kept my distance." She scratched her head and then looked at the ground. "She's still my mom."

She was trying to convince herself that it was okay to have a conversation with her mom without falling back into the trap, that was their relationship. I hated her feeling like this and to be honest it was starting to piss me off.

"You sure?"

"Yeah baby, I'm good." She looked at me and I pecked her on the lips.

I was still skeptical of how she was feeling but I would be right there with her and if things went sideways, won't nobody be happy. Once we were both presentable I grabbed her hand and we walked in the living room where her mom and Darren were sitting on the couch. I pulled her over to the recliner I bought for her a few weeks ago and pulled her down on my lap. She curled up and looked ahead.

"How you doing Lala?" Darren was the first person to speak.

"I'm okay, Lake woke up so now it's just getting everything together for him to be able to come home. We're going to see him tomorrow."

"Good, I'm glad to hear that baby girl." He nodded his head and then an uncomfortable silence filled the room. The more the tension grew the more pissed I got. I was trying to stay out of it but I've never been fond of Cynt.

"So, what brings y'all by?" I cut right to the chase, no need in sitting here taking up air.

"I—I" Cynt stuttered, Darren grabbed her hand and she looked at him and smiled. For as long as I've known her I have never saw her smile like that at Lala or even acknowledge her enough to make her think she cared. "I wanted, no I needed to come and talk to you baby," she gave Lala her attention. "I know that I wasn't there for you when your dad died. I know that I turned into a monster. I will never be able to forgive myself for the things that I've said and done to you. I went to rehab and I even started counseling to be able to get over everything that happened."

She smiled but Lala's face was stone cold. I encased her in my arms and she laid her head on my shoulder. I could feel the warm tears touching my collar bone and it burned me up to think that someone who was supposed to love her unconditionally could just turn that love off because life didn't go the way she wanted it to.

"Why wasn't I good enough?" Lala all but whispered.

"Don't you ever say that again," I shrugged my shoulder so that she sat up and looked me in the face. "You are more than enough, if someone doesn't see that shit then they're a got damn fool. Don't ever say that shit again and I mean it. She was the problem not you." I pointed at her mother. "She had the fucked-up mind frame not you. You did everything that you were supposed to do plus some so don't you ever try and take on someone else's burdens."

"You don't think I know that Heart? I know what I've done and how that affected her. I know that now. I don't need you to outline that in her mind. I'm trying to fix things with my daughter. I've never done anything to *you* for *you* to even be commenting on the situation."

"No, you've never done anything to me directly, but every time this girl is hurt because of something you did or something you said it took a piece of me too. I love her that much! I love her more than you could ever fathom and I know that shit for a fact because if you did we wouldn't even be sitting here right now having this conversation." I could feel myself getting upset and so could La because she put her hand on my chest and it comforted me just a little. "Her heartbeat is my heartbeat and every time you stomped on hers mine stopped for her."

"Baby," Lala tried to stop me but I wasn't done so I ignored her advance.

"And if you ain't serious about fixing shit with her, if you doing this just to ease your conscious, if you plan on throwing her to the wayside after you fix yourself then I suggest you take your ass on somewhere now because when it comes down to it I won't see her hurt behind you again."

"Is that a threat?"

"It's whatever the fuck you want it to be." I sat back in the chair and wrapped my arms around La's waist. She turned and kissed me on the lips and let it linger. I loved La more than any words could ever describe and that was a dangerous feeling especially to those who try and hurt that in anyway.

Cynt sighed heavily because she looked over in our direction. "I deserve that," she nodded her head and La sat up.

"Excuse me?" Hell, I wanted her to say that shit again. The last five years that I've gotten to experience Cynt hasn't been the most pleasant so to hear her own up to her shit was mind blowing even to me.

"Oh, you heard me," she waved her hand up in the air. "I was a horrible mother to you Laurence these last five years and I hate myself for it. I really do. And I'm so sorry baby. I swear that I will spend the rest of my life making up for the shit I've done, I want you to know that." The tears where flowing on both La and Cynt's face. "And Heart there are no words to show my gratitude for what you did for the both of us during all of this. I'm so glad that she had you in her corner. Everything you said to me was true and I can put it on my life that I will be the best mother and grandmother I can be."

"Wait I'm not pregnant." Lala looked at me with confusion written on her face and shrugged my shoulders because I didn't know what the fuck she was talking about either.

"Child you may not be pregnant yet but the way that man got you glowing, it's coming." Cynt threw her hands up and then smiled in Lala's direction. She was laughing and so was I.

"Mom I missed you so much." La said hopping off of my lap and running over to her mother. I watched as the two embraced and I was satisfied with it. I knew that deep down this is what La wanted. "I got one question though." She pulled back. "Were you and Uncle D messing around on Daddy?" she looked back and forth between the two of them.

"Lala you know me better than that, when I say your daddy was my brother he was just that. I would never betray him. Me and your mother just kind of happened, it wasn't planned. When I came back to town I came solely to find y'all and see how y'all were, never in a million years did I think that I would walk into what I did. The minute I saw your mom like she was my heart hurt and I felt like I failed your dad. He told me to look after y'all and I didn't so I made it my business to fix that and that was my only goal. I never thought that during the process that I would fall for your mother the way I did. If you have an issue with it let us know."

"He's right baby, we both left you when you needed us the most so if this makes you uncomfortable then we will end it. I won't lie, it's gonna be hard because I love him but we owe you that and so much more."

The room grew quiet and everyone was just waiting on La's answer and reaction to what was just said. I believe them that they weren't fucking around behind Big L's back and from the smile on La's face so did she.

"No mom you deserve to be happy and I'm kinda happy it's Uncle D." She smiled. "Just don't ever leave me again, either one of you."

"I'll put that on my life." Darren said.

"Now I need to catch up on all things Laurence, tell me what's been going on. How's school been going?" Cynt asked. They engaged in a conversation about everything that's been going on.

"Aye let me holla at you outside." Darren said and looked back at Cynt and La as they talked and caught up on each other. I nodded my head and headed to the back to grab my gun, I tucked it in the back of my shorts and followed him out the door but not before I kissed La and told her where I was going.

The air was brisk and the stars filled the sky perfectly like it was some kind of painting. It was a perfect night. Shit was lining up, there was only one thing left to do and that was to take care of Mitch's bitch ass.

"Aye what the fuck you do to that nigga at the police station?"

"What you talking about?" Darren laughed.

"Man, that nigga was mad as fuck talking about some pictures. I almost beat his got damn ass in that room." I shook my head.

"Me and Big L always kept a set of insurances. That's how we were able to move like we did, if anyone tried to come near us we kept some shit to make sure we stayed safe. I never stopped getting that insurance." He smirked. "Tell me about this Mitch nigga. Detective Ringo is my nigga and we go way back. He used to keep shit on lock for me and Big L and he say this nigga Mitch is a major fucking problem."

"Ringo, that shit sound familiar as fuck." I thought about where I had heard the name before and then it hit me, that's the cop that Mitch said was after him that day Menks got hemmed up. "That's the cop that's after Mitch real bad. What's up with that?"

"He killed his partner because he sent him to look into info on Big L's killer."

I stared at him and grit my back teeth. I had mad respect for Big L because he made it possible for us to eat and he treated us like family. One of the main reasons I latched on to La the way I did in the beginning was because I felt like I owed that nigga. I just didn't expect to fall in love with her.

"So that nigga gone die for more than one reason?"

"Looks like it, let me holla at my nigga Ringo to see exactly what happened and then it's all on you. He shot me a text a while ago saying he had info. Another reason I needed to come here. I didn't know if it was a good idea to tell Lala or not but Cynt knows."

"Let me tell her if Cynt didn't already tell her."

"Yo who the fuck is that creeping and shit?" Darren said and pointed and there was a navy-blue Ford Explorer with tinted windows headed out way. "Yo get down!" Darren yelled but the car had already started bussing. I pulled out my gun and started letting off rounds.

I made sure I got a good look at the passenger and it was lil Jay's bitch ass. He had just signed his death certificate with his bitch ass uncle. I continued to shoot until my gun was empty, by then the truck had already sped out of the creek.

"Yo D you good?" I said noticing that he had retreated back further into the building.

"Yeah man just a graze," he was holding his shoulder that housed a big ass hole, looked like the bullet went through and through but his ass was leaking.

"Graze my fucking ass, you need to go to the hospital."

"Darren!" Cynt came tearing down the stairs.

"Baby!" I could hear the worry in Lala's voice, I met her at the end of the stairs and grabbed her up. She was shaking but she had her gun in her hand. *My girl!* "Oh no Darren you're shot!"

"I'm good baby girl, did you see who the fuck did this?" Darren said voice full of venom."

"Yep!" was all I said. "La go pack some clothes we can't stay here until this shit boil over. We got to go to a hotel." My number one priority was to make sure that La was safe and her being here wasn't safe in my opinion.

"Hell no," Darren spoke up. "I just bought a crib out in Curtis Pond, y'all can stay with us until we handle this shit. Go get your stuff."

La looked at me and I nodded my head. She ran up the stairs to get our things and Cynt went to help her. I had to go to my apartment to get a few things while I was at it but we were gonna go together. I didn't feel right leaving her here. Shit had just got real and I was ready to light the fucking streets up, I just needed to get my girl safe.

CHAPTER 14

*M**iracle*

The shots could be heard throughout the creek, out of habit I ducked down. Stray bullets have no eyes so I wasn't about to risk being shot. That was the one thing I hated about staying in the hood. Gunshots were normal. I waited until the gunfire stopped, before I headed outside to be nosey.

The hood had its downfall's but there was upsides too, one being that everything that goes down is buzzing in the streets within minutes. By the time I get to the green box it's guaranteed that they will know who was shooting and who they were shooting at.

Slipping on my flip flops and grabbing my phone and keys I headed out side. The cool air hit my face and I instantly regretted not grabbing a jacket. I looked up the street then back down, just like I suspected it was busy.

Lately I had been holed up in my house. I had passed my state boards a month ago and was working out of a local shop here in Mooresville. Besides going to work, I was home. I hadn't been up to see Lake in a few days, not since I walked in on him saying that he didn't love me and I only wore his last name because he was scared I was gonna snitch on him.

To say I was hurt was an understatement, I couldn't even describe what I felt when I heard those words come out of his mouth. I was so mad that I couldn't even cry, I just backed away from the door and came home and I hadn't been back since.

The fucked-up part about the whole thing was that I loved him more than anything and I hated myself for that because when it came down to it, I knew I deserved better. I just thought that he would give me better when he got his situation under control.

Most would think that I was dumb getting with a man that was in a relationship but no one knew the loyalty that I had for this man and the only reason I had that loyalty was because I thought he had the same for me. I was slowly starting to under-stand that it was all bullshit.

I had to shake my head as everything was starting to make sense with our whole relationship. I kept trying to make myself not jump to conclusions and give him a chance to speak for himself but it was hard when you look at everything around us.

Admitting that I was stupid was something that I was strug-gling with. Hell, I was struggling with this whole situation. Shit wasn't what I thought it was, and to think I lost my best friend over this shit.

"Heyyyyyy Miracle, what's up girl?" Maaze one of the local

dealers called out to me. He had just got out of jail a few months ago and the nigga was fine, not your average fine but he had a swag about him that made you want to be in his presence.

"What's good Maaze?"

"Not shit, niggas out here acting a fool and shit." He nodded towards the top of the creek.

"At the top?" My heart quickened, I hoped that Lala was okay. I don't know what I would do if something happened to her. I grabbed my stomach and was about to take off towards the top of the creek but I saw Heart's Impala come barreling down the bottom of the creek.

I watched as Heart jumped out of the car with blood on him and that set off all kinds of alarms. I ran to the car and looked inside, I met Lala's stare as soon as I looked in the passenger seat. I ran over and swung the door open and grabbed her hand.

"What you doing Miracle?" she asked me.

"Whose blood is on Hearts shirt?" I continued to look her over despite the mug on her face. Once I was satisfied that nothing was wrong with her I pulled her into me and hugged her. For a while I was hugging by myself then all of a sudden, I felt her arms around me. I couldn't help the tears that fell and the sobs that escaped my lips. I missed my friend, my sister.

"Don't cry." She rubbed my back.

"This baby got my ass emotional as hell." I said laughing and her body became rigid at the mention of the baby. I slowly removed my arms from around her and she just stared at me. "I just wanted to make sure that you were okay."

"Miracle you have to see how fucked up this situation is for me." She looked at me with pleading eyes. She wanted me to understand how she was feeling but I was the one married to a man that didn't love me like he said he did and now I'm pregnant with his kid. No, she was being so selfish right now.

"You're selfish as fuck, I'm so confused as to why you think any of this has to do with you. Every conversation we've had you keep talking about how this affects you, and what this is doing to you. Lala what about the people that are actually apart of this whole big ass mess?

"That you caused!" she yelled at me and I had to laugh to keep from swinging on my sister.

"So, I got into bed with myself? I went to that courthouse and I married myself? I carried on a two-year relationship by my got damn self!" I yelled. "Oh okay!" I shook my head and went to turn around to leave.

"Why couldn't you just leave him alone? Now everything is all fucked up. You should have just left him alone." The tears that fell didn't phase me because she was still judging a situation that she didn't know anything about.

"You can't help who you love, right?"

"But he played you Miracle, I didn't want you to have to go through that. Lake is a liar and he doesn't love you. He loves Mira and I promise you that's who he was going to be with. No matter what happens he will not be with you Miracle I just want you to know that. I don't want you to have to go through that hurt which is why I wanted you to stay away. I love you too much to watch you go through this. You may think it's selfish of me but it is what it is.

This is wrong and no one is gonna win, I promise you that."

Her words stung, she was right. No one was going to win but I wasn't about to let her know what I was feeling. This shit was getting painful, I was about to walk away until Maaze walked over with the scoop.

"Yo they say Lil Jay and Jason was up there shooting in the top, when they pulled out they got stopped and they dumb asses had drugs and them dumb ass girls with them. They all going down for that shit."

"Fuck!" Heart said. "Aye yo Maaze hit me up if that nigga get out though. I gotta bullet with his name on it."

"Bet that nigga, stay up," he nodded his head and glanced my way as he made his way back to the green box. I shook my head and headed to my car. I wasn't in the mood to be judged by La today. I needed a break from all negativity.

I walked to my car and hopped in, it wasn't anything special but it got me to work and back and I was proud of it. I got it right before Lake got shot and it was one of the things that was positive in my life.

Hopping in I turned on Medicine by Queen Naija, the words of this song resonated with me. I shut out the world and sung the words of how I was feeling.

Swear I cannot win for losing
I been out here being faithful
I always got this on lockdown
But that ain't been keeping us stable

So I guess I know what I gotta do
Give you a taste of your own medicine (hey, yeah)

Before I knew it, the tears were falling from my eyes and I couldn't control them. As bad as I wanted them to stop they wouldn't. I was in love with a man that didn't give a fuck about me and no matter how bad I wanted to think that he would somehow tell me that what I heard was wrong I knew the truth.

I had been faithful to a man that wouldn't give up a seat on the bus for me. I knew better. How did I let him enter my heart and tear that shit all the way down? I always told myself that I would never be like my mother and that's exactly who I was. Her made all over.

Shaking my head at myself, I had a lot going for me. I had a career and I had plans and goals. I didn't deserve this but Lala was right, I brought this shit on myself. I knew what I had to do, I was done being a fool.

Pulling up to the hood store I hoped out. The hood store was a store owed by this cool ass Arabian dude and it was connected to Dyson square. Everybody came through here because he had everything and he sold loosies (single cigarettes) and 12oz beers for a dollar. You couldn't beat the prices at the hood store.

I was craving a pickled egg and a hot weenie and I knew he kept a fresh jar so I pulled up and got out. I went in and got what I came to get and got ready to walk out of the store. Not paying attention I ran right into somebody and when I looked up it was the bitch that showed up at Waffle House and the hospital.

"You should watch where you're going bitch!"

"No bitch you should back the fuck up," I hissed. "You better be glad I'm pregnant or I would whoop your fucking ass." I pushed passed her.

"Probably don't even know who the fuck your baby daddy is." She said under her breath but I heard what she said.

"Oh, this is my husband's baby, yeah bitch you heard it right, *my husband!*

She didn't say anything she just walked up closer to me and raised her foot but before I could react she kicked me and I doubled over in pain. I couldn't hit her back, I couldn't do anything but hold my belly and pray.

"Oh my god, somebody call 911!" I could hear someone yell out. The next sound I heard was heels clicking and people rushing over to where I was. I was in so much pain that I could barely breathe.

Why didn't I just leave it alone? I should have just went home. Why in the hell did I have to stand there and argue with that bitch? *God please don't let me lose my baby.*

"Is that Miracle?" I heard Lala's voice yell out. "Oh no Miracle! What the fuck happened to her?"

"That lady right there that's pulling off in that red car, she kicked her in the stomach."

"Who the fuck is that?" I heard Lala ask.

"Mitch's wife Wynn, Lake was fucking with her."

When I heard Heart say that I really broke down. All of this was because Lake didn't love anyone but himself. I lost my baby because I believed that he loved me. I cried until I heard the ambulance pull up and whisk me off to the hospital.

"She's pregnant." I heard Lala say to the EMS as she climbed on the ambulance with me. I had yet to open my eyes, I was scared that if I opened my eyes then what was going on would be my reality and right now not thinking about that was getting me through this pain.

～

"*A*re you okay?" I heard the room door open and I shut my eyes real tight because I wasn't in the mood. I was hoping that Lala would think that I was sleep and just leave but I should have knew better. "Bitch I know you not sleep! When you sleep you do that twitching shit and you ain't doing it so stop playing with me."

I giggled a little for the first time today. She was right my fingers had a mind of their own when I was sleep. Only people knew that was Lala and Lake. Just the thought of him brought a sadness over me and I could feel the tears coming.

"I just want to be alone."

"Oh well, because we need to talk."

"I don't want to hear your I told you so's Lala so you can keep them. I already know that Lake ain't shit." The tears found their way to my cheeks and I didn't bother to stop them.

"I owe you an apology," that caused me to sit up in the bed and give her my undivided attention. "I haven't been a really good friend to you. Now I don't apologize for my position on the situation because I still think that you and Lake are dead ass wrong but I am sorry for how I handled you. You are my best friend; my sister and I was so wrapped up on trying to make sure that everyone saw me as a loyal person that I stopped being loyal to my friend. For that I'm so sorry girl."

She threw her arms around me and I let her, we hugged and both cried our eyes out. This is what I've wanted through all of this. My friend, I understood that she thought I was wrong but just to know that she's here for me right or wrong is all I wanted from her.

"That's all I wanted from you La, that's it. To know that you were riding for me just like I would ride for you. Right or wrong."

"I get that and seeing you laying on the ground in all that blood opened my eyes to that shit. Just thinking about losing you made me realize that shit ain't perfect and people fuck up, hell I fuck up and my ass can't run around judging people when I'm not in their shoes. Lesson learned."

"You were right though." I said sadly.

"About what?"

"Lake, I overheard him telling Mira that he only married me to make sure that I didn't snitch on him but how could that be when he knew just like anyone else that I would never do that? I'm not built that way. Just like now, what's so different now? I could go tell that shit now then what?" I shrugged my shoulders. "Hell, him marrying me didn't change shit anyway." I took the back on my hand and wiped my face.

"No because hell, no one fucking knew, hell if you ask anyone he's married to Mira."

"Exactly! Thinking back, I was dumb as hell. I swear I hung

on to that man's every word. If I didn't hear it with my own ears I would have never believed that he didn't love me." I looked up at La and for the first time since all of this started and she had sympathy in them for me.

"Love makes us do some crazy shit." We both chuckled.

"Yeah, La but y'all don't get it, he told me that he didn't love her and that we were gonna be together as soon as his kids were old enough to understand. He made me believe that at the end of the day, no matter what it looked like from the outside, it was just me and him and I believed him Lala."

"Miracle you made yourself believe that you could change him when in reality you can't change a man because you want him to be something that he's not." I covered my face with my hands and wailed like never before, I needed to get it out because after this a lot was gonna change for me. "Gotta stop trying to paint people who already showed you their true colors, you'll always end up with a mess."

"Through all of this I wanted my baby though."

"I know you did but everything happens for a reason, God shut this door so he can open up a bigger and better one." She kissed my cheek and a tear rolled down my face. I held my empty stomach and thought about everything that I had been through. I would never want to bring a baby into that anyway.

CHAPTER 15

M *itch*

"How in the fuck did you end up in fucking jail Jay?" I yelled through the receiver. I had told him and Jason to go and take care of Heart. I told him where he was and what to do. Somehow this dumb ass ended up in jail. I swear I think his mama dropped his ass on his head when he was young or maybe she snorted too much coke, hell it was something because this nigga is dumb as shit.

"Unc we did what you said but the nigga wasn't by his self, some old nigga was with him and they both was busting back. Shit we didn't know what to do so we burnt out. The police pulled us over right outside the creek."

"Why in the fuck did you have drugs on you?"

"You told us to do the drop."

"Nigga that was yesterday!" I ran my hand over my head. I

don't know what the fuck I was thinking having them do anything.

"Shit came up, look just get us out of here," he said.

"I don't know if I can, you had them fucking girls with you." I fussed. "I'll see what I can do but you gone have to sit for a few."

"Man, Unc don't leave us in here." I hung up the phone and threw myself in the chair in my office. What the fuck was going on right now? Nothing was moving right, Chief Shriel was on my ass and I had other shit going on.

I was cutting my product and making side deals out from under Wyndel and he didn't know it. I needed the money because I was trying to take him out soon, hell I was gone have to because if I found out for sure that Wynn was fucking around on me I was gone kill her ass.

The conversation with her and Mira at the restaurant played over and over in my mind and then the shit with her and Mello. Every time I asked her she would deny it but the shit just wasn't adding up.

I did my thing but I loved my wife and I honestly believed that she loved me too which was why I was gonna do my own investigation before I jump to any conclusion. It would definitely be deadly so I was moving smart.

I heard the front door open and shut, Wynn came running upstairs and the look on her face was one that I couldn't read. It was like she was worried, scared and pissed off all at the same time.

"What's wrong with you?" I asked her and she just looked at

me and shook her head like she didn't want to talk. The shit that she had been pulling didn't give her the option not to talk. So, I grabbed her arm and pulled her to me.

"Mitch please, I just got into it with someone and they got me feeling some kind of way. We got so much going on and I keep finding myself taking my anger out on other people. I just flipped out on some bitch, I'm fine though." She flashed an uneasy smile that didn't sit well with me.

"Well who was it that you attacked?"

"Got damn it Mitch just let it go! I just want a shower and a stiff ass drink. Let me have that," she fussed as she stomped up the stairs.

She was really on some bullshit. I went to the bar and made myself a drink and then copped a seat on the couch. I was supposed to be living the good life right now. I took down one of the biggest drug dealers that this side of the US had ever seen and I took over his territory. Life should be great for me right now.

Instead I'm going to war with two of my toughest soldiers, my wife is out here running the streets like she's fucking single and my supplier is my father in law. I was fucked every which a way you look at it.

There was a knock at the door and I looked at my phone and clicked the app for the security system, saw it was Mello and went to open the door. When it opened he looked past me and I was about to address him until I saw two police cars pull up in the front of my yard.

"What the fuck?" I said more to myself than to Mello but he had an answer.

"Yo they saying that Wynn kicked Lake's wife in the stomach and caused her to miscarry. I just left the hood store, they got that shit taped off and one of the girls said that ol' dude that run the store gave the police the tapes."

"Why in the fuck would she do some shit like that?"

"That's what the fuck I want to know." Mello's voice was full of jealousy and hurt like Wynn was his damn wife. The more I start to think about shit the more suspect they start to look. I glared at him but he was paying me no attention. His attention was focused on what was behind me.

When I turned to meet his stare, Wynn was walking down the stairs. I looked at Mello who had a mug on his face and when he saw me looking at him he didn't bother to change it. He shook his head and walked off. *This nigga was getting bold!*

"Who's at the door?" she asked from the stairs.

"I don't know, come find out." I said and walked away as she walked up. When she saw it was the police she glanced my way but I didn't give a fuck how the shit looked. She was a half second away from the grave so if she knew what I knew then she would be thankful for the police.

"Really Mitch?"

"Yeah, call Mello." I said and her eyes stretched telling me what I needed to know. Wynn never was a good liar, she was a sneaky bitch but she couldn't lie worth shit.

"No, I'll just call daddy." She threw back at me.

"Yeah bitch do that too." I shrugged and headed for the stairs, she was on her own and I was about to see what I could do to make sure that her and Mello pay for this shit. Some shit was going on and I was about to find out what it was and handle that shit. Then I was getting the fuck out of town. Maybe somewhere on the west coast.

I needed to make a few phone calls. Just in case I had to make a move I needed my ass covered. picking up the phone I dialed Shriel's number.

"Thank you for calling the Mooresville Police Department, how can I direct your call?"

"I'm trying to reach Chief Shriel." I said confused as to why his personal number went to the police station.

"Chief Shriel is no longer with us, he was transferred to another precinct. I can connect you to Chief Ringo if you would like."

I immediately hung up the phone, what the fuck just happened? Shit was getting thick around here. After dealing with these snakes I was out of here.

CHAPTER 16

*L*ake
     I had been calling Mira every day since the day she
left here telling me that we were over. We had been
together for over seven years and she thought that we could just
be over like that? I don't think so and I wasn't about to be okay
with it. I know I fucked up but hell everybody fuck up every now
and then.

One thing about me though, I could promise that it would
never happen again. As soon as I could get in contact with Miracle, who wasn't answering the phone either I would talk her into
getting an abortion. She was playing hardball right now but I
knew her and she loved me enough to do what the fuck I said.

"Yooooo!" Heart said as he stepped in my room. I was ready
to get out of this muthafucka and I couldn't wait till tomorrow,

hell I might not even wait. I might just bust myself out tonight. What the fuck is one day?

"What's good my nigga?"

"Nigga you got problems." Heart said as he slouched down in the chair that sat across the room from the hospital bed that had been my home for over a month.

"What's up?"

"First nigga, Wynn ass kicked Miracle in the stomach and she lost the baby."

Call me a heartless ass nigga but I wasn't sad about that shit. That was God's way of telling me that I was supposed to be with Mira. That was my muthafuckin sign. I couldn't help the smile that spread across my face. I couldn't help the feeling of happiness that crept in my heart.

"She okay?"

"Nigga you ask that shit after you was sitting there smiling and shit like you just hit the lottery? You need to get your shit together because you caused all of this shit. And that baby didn't have nothing to do with this." I could tell he was getting heated and I wasn't about to get into with my boy because of my fuck ups.

"You right, I'm tripping but I didn't want that baby and she knew it. That baby complicated shit for me so I won't sit here and pretend to be sad about the shit. You know me better than that my G." He nodded his head saying that he understood me but that didn't wipe the mug that was plastered on his face.

"Mira back fucking with Jaxson."

"Come again?"

"Nigga you heard me." He shifted in his seat.

"Since fucking when?"

"That I can't tell you but the day you woke up we stopped by to holla at Mira and he was there with her. She told us to mind our fucking business."

"And you just now telling me?"

"Nigga I was too busy getting fucking shot at to remember to tell you that yo girl moved the fuck on." He stood up and headed towards the door. My nigga had the weight of the world on his shoulders and I wasn't helping. I was bitching about something that I caused. "Yo you need to go check on Miracle she's in the ER, they releasing her in a few. And when you talk to Mira, act like you got some got damn sense."

I didn't say a word I just nodded my head. I knew that if I went over there to the house that I paid for and there was a nigga there I was flipping the fuck out so I wasn't about to lie to my nigga. I had done too much of that shit.

I got up and headed to the bathroom to piss, I had started walking better with the help of physical therapy. I could handle all my hygiene shit and I passed all of their little fucked up test so they said that I could go home and I was happy as hell. I still had to do physical therapy but that was too be expected.

Walking past the nurses station I told them where I was going, they insisted that I take a wheel chair but I refused and walked off while they were still talking. I took the elevator down to the ER and tried to prepare myself for this conversation.

I knew it wasn't good. I was sure that Miracle heard the conversation that me and Mira had and that was more than likely why I hadn't heard from her. She was ducking a nigga hard. I just hoped she didn't give me a hard time about this marriage.

Miracle wasn't that type of girl to do the whole revenge shit because a man didn't want her, she was better than that and she would for sure move on. I didn't know how I felt about another nigga being in my space with her but if that's what it took to get Mira back then I would do just that.

Walking in her room, her and Lala was hugged up and that shit made me happy. I hated that they had fell out because of me. I didn't want them at odds because of my fuck ups. When La looked up at me she had a scowl on her face, she wasn't my biggest fan right now and rightfully so.

Not only was this fucking up my life it was interfering with the people that was closest to us. Once all of this shit blew over I would make it up to all of them.

"I'm gonna let you talk to him." The distain that fell from the word him hurt a little bit. La had always been sis to me. Now she acted like she didn't want anything to do with me. "I'll be down the hall, I'll go see about your discharge papers." Miracle nodded her head and then watched La leave.

The tension in the air was suffocating and caused me to be uncomfortable. I cleared my throat and Miracle looked my way. She had this far off look in her eyes, it was almost cold. Her disheveled hair fell down her back, she was in some Carolina blue hospital scrubs with Lake Norman Reginal Hospital written on the pocket.

They must have given them to her because her clothes were

all bloody. I really felt bad about all of this but shit happens and now it's time to make shit right.

"How you feeling?" I tried to break the ice but when she scoffed I knew the tone that the conversation was headed before we even got started.

"What do you want Lake, why are you even here?" she rolled her eyes at me.

"I want to check on you. Damn I can't do that?"

"Why do you want to check on me now, because I'm your wife? Huh?" she released a frustrated laugh. "Oh, you're just coming to make sure the baby is really dead. Humph!"

"Don't say no shit like that."

"Nigga it's the truth and I know you're happy so you can go to hell with this little act you got going on." She waved her hands in the air and I just stared at her for a minute. I could still see the shape of her body through the big scrubs, Miracle was sexy and that's what drew me to her. That and the way she loved me.

When things with me and Mira went south I always knew that I could come to Miracle and she would make shit okay. That used to be Mira until we had the kids, I wasn't jealous of my kids, I knew they need all of the attention and I loved the fact that Mira did to. So, when I found Miracle I had the best of both worlds but my heart was at home with my family.

"You know like I know that this is what's best for all involved."

"No, you selfish son of a bitch it's what's best for you. You don't care about me and you don't care about Mira. All you care about is what is making Lake happy for the moment. Tell me something did you ever love me?"

I was dreading this question, it was something that I never talked about with her. She would tell me that she loved me all the time but I never returned it because I didn't feel the same way. I treated her well and I showed her that I cared about her but I only loved Mira, I guess it was time to be honest about that.

"Miracle I care about you, and I got mad love for you but—"

"Get out!" she pointed at the door.

"Listen, I'm trying to be honest. Just hear me out."

"You should have been honest with me a year ago when you stood before me and God and promised to love and honor me for the rest of your fucking life. I let you be you, I never tried to change you because I knew in my heart of hearts that it would be me and you in the end. Ain't that what you told me? That it would be me and you till the end."

"I'm sorry."

"Tell me something I don't know nigga." And there goes that mouth. "You made me believe that there was a future with you. That was the only reason I sit back and let you handle Mira the way that you did. If I had known the truth then I would have never done that shit Lake.

"Did you really think this marriage was for real? I mean come on Miracle. I lived with Mira, I fucked Mira, she has my kids. Anytime anyone saw me out it was with Mira. When I took you out we had to go out of town. Didn't that tell you something? I mean come on."

"That's because you told me that the kids—"

"Miracle stop lying to yourself, you knew what it was. I married you because I had to."

"Yeah and you need to stop lying to yourself Lake, you knew I would do anything for you so why would I snitch you out? You married me because you wanted me to stay with you knowing that you were with Mira. I see that shit now and I'm good on it and you." She pointed at me. "The baby is dead and we have no ties, you can leave."

"We have ties Miracle, you just—"

"I said get out."

"We need to talk about this Miracle you can't just—"

"GET THE FUCK OUT NOOOOOOWWWWWWWW!"

She screamed and wouldn't listen to anything else I had to say. She was done and I couldn't blame her. As soon as I got out of here, I was filing for divorce and working on my relationship with Mira. First things first was to get that nigga Jaxson away from her.

ira

Lake had been calling me nonstop, I never answered the phone nor did I text him back. You would think that he would get the message but he didn't. I received a text saying that he was stopping by to see the kids when he got out of the hospital and that we needed to talk.

I knew that it was wrong of me to keep the kids away from him because he was their father but I didn't want to be around him right now. Laken and Larken ask about him all the time. They want to know why daddy don't live in the same house as us and as bad as I want to tell them the truth I just don't have the heart to do that.

In a fantasy world I would just forgive Lake and we could move on and live happily ever after but in reality, in my real life I know that I'll never trust him again. Not after everything he's done.

Loving Lake is something that I will always do but the in-love part faded when I found him cheating on me in the front seat of our car and then it diminished when I found out that he was married to his side chick.

How can someone get past that and how in the hell did he expect me to? I think I could forgive him I just didn't know if I could forgive him enough to be with him.

"Mommmmmyyyyyy!" I heard Larken yell through the house. "Daddy and uncle Heart are here." That little girl was definitely my child, she was loud as shit. "Laken, daddy here."

"Daddddddyyyyy!" I could hear him yell and come tearing down the stairs.

By the time the both of them were in the foyer I could hear Lake attempting to put his key in the door. I laughed because to me it was funny that he thought he would still have access. He may have been paying for the house but my credit got us the house and it was in my name. So, I changed the locks.

Laken reached up and unlocked the door. "What have I told you about opening the door Laken? Huh?" I fussed as the door swung open.

"He was opening it up for me and why don't my key work?"

"Because you no longer live here." I rolled my eyes and headed back in the living room where I was sitting going through the paper looking for a job. While Lake was taking care of every-thing I went back to school online a few years ago and got my

Medical Transcription degree and I was glad I did. I was about to put that degree to use.

"How you gone kick me out of a house that I pay for?"

"And that you will continue to pay for. Your kids live here and I'm not packing them up and moving them because their daddy is a—" I stopped when I realized that Laken and Larken were standing there hanging on to every word. I hated to fight in front of them, that's the one thing that I promised myself that I wouldn't do and that was let them see us fight.

They would come to understand that mommy and daddy wouldn't be together anymore but it didn't have to be ugly and we would love them the same.

"Hey, go upstairs and play for a second while I talk to mommy." He said looking back and forth between the twins.

"Aye yo Laken I bet I whoop yo ass in 2K." Heart said and I flashed him a look that said watch your mouth and he laughed per usual. They took off back up the stairs with Heart promising Larken that he would play tea party while he plays with Laken on the game.

Once they were out of ear shot I sat down to have this conversation with Lake, it was long overdue but it needed to be said.

"So, you want me to pay for this house for you and yo nigga?" Was the first thing out of his mouth.

"That's what this is about?" I shook my head. "You worried about Jaxson? Someone who has been there for me through all the bullshit you put me through? The bitch in your car and you being married? You worried about that?"

"When you start fucking that nigga? Before or after you found out I made a mistake."

"Ha! A mistake? A fucking mistake is forgetting to put gas in my car after you drove all of it out, not you being married and fucking bitches." I yelled unintentionally. "Jaxson has been nothing but a gentlemen to me, he hasn't tried me once. Not even when I damn near threw the pussy at him. He told me that I was better than that, that I deserved more than that and he's right." The tears started to fall involuntarily. "He said that he knew that I loved you and he wouldn't interfere with that until I completely closed that door. So, unlike you I haven't opened my legs for anybody."

"Got damn Mira a nigga made a mistake. I ain't perfect! What you think you gone get with that nigga and everything gone be all good? That nigga probably gone cheat too."

"Why because I'm not good enough to be faithful to?"

"No that's not what I'm saying, what I'm saying is sometimes a man has to figure out how special what he has at home is. I know that now."

"You sound just as dumb as you look right now."

"Mira listen, I'll chill and it will be just you and me from this point forward."

"I don't trust that no more than I trust you. Lake you had something good, we had something good. We weren't perfect and I'm sure there was some things that I need to work on within myself and like you said you ain't perfect but that's what communication is all about. You don't go out fucking random bitches and you don't go out and get whole wives."

"I'm getting a divorce, I told you why I had to marry her."

"And I told you that you were a bold face lie." I shook my head because he was still sitting here trying to paint me this picture when I already seen the real thing.

"I'm trying to right my wrongs."

"Well right them for you, because I'm done. If I took you back I would be constantly wondering where you were or what you were doing. Anytime you went to the creek I would have to be right there with you and if you slipped up and went by yourself I would swear that you were with her. Don't you see? What kind of way is that to live for either of us? I don't want to have to check your phone and social media or make you share your location so I can know that you are where you say you are. I don't want that."

He didn't say anything it was like he was pondering over what I said and he needed to. I was serious, I was not about to live like my career was a Private Investigator. Fuck that. I want to be able to trust my man and I couldn't have that with Lake.

"You could grow to trust me again."

"You think I will ever forget that there was someone out there with your last name and it wasn't me?" I rested my elbows on my thighs and let my hands hang over my knees. I just wanted him to understand where I was coming from. "Let's be honest, with the line of work you're in and the type of person you are. You would be miserable living like that. After a while you would grow to resent me and I would resent you for being selfish enough to take me through that after everything that you already took me through." I let the tears fall freely.

"Mira, I love you and I'm so sorry. I just want to make this right." He pleaded.

"If you love me you would let me go and let me be happy. That's the only way to make this right. I need time to heal and I can't do that with you all in my face. I need space and I need for you to understand that even though I love you, there is no more us."

"You think I'm just gone sit back and watch you run off into the sunset with that nigga though? That ain't happening."

"So, what you gone kill every nigga I come in contact with?" I put my hand under my chin like I was thinking. "What's that gonna solve? Besides you going to jail and not being in your kids life. Cause it won't make me want to be with you again."

"Why won't you just listen to me Mira? I love you baby. I don't want to live in a house without you in the kids."

"You are so selfish, because you don't want to live in a house without us you want me to be miserable and in turn your kids will be miserable all because you want what you want. Think about what you're saying Lake. Everything is I, I, I... think about someone other than you and your dick."

"You think the kids don't want me here?"

"Oh no I know they do but they don't understand what's going on. They're five, but they know that mommy's sad and they hate it. Don't make that a permanent thing in their life. Let me go, there's nothing else there."

He stared at me in my eyes for the longest time and didn't say anything. After a while he dropped his head and let it hang.

Then all of a sudden, he stood up and took the stairs two at a time. I could hear him upstairs with the kids.

I knew this was gone be a long road ahead of me but I knew I was better than this situation and I couldn't be what Lake wanted me to be for him anymore. He had to be that for himself and I had to find what I need for me. I just knew that it wasn't him.

CHAPTER 18

W ynn

"I can't believe he just left me in jail like that." I fussed while folding myself into Mello's body. He was always my go to when it wasn't Lake. I had actually started to grow feelings for him and I knew he had some for me, I could tell by his actions.

He had got to the point that he didn't care about what Mitch thought or felt anymore. He had started popping up at the house and he's been stuck to me like glue. Especially since the baby.

I was pregnant but it wasn't Mitch's, hell I didn't even know if it was Mello's. In my heart I knew it was Lake's which was why I got so mad when I heard that bitch say that she was pregnant with her husband's baby. That shit took me to another level and I had one thing on my mind and that was to kick the baby out of her.

Getting as angry as I did hadn't happen to me in a long time but it happened that night. I put my hand over my stomach and Mello followed my gesture. I didn't want him to get excited because I didn't know if I was having this baby or not. If he knew how many I've already killed he'd probably kill me himself.

"I told you to just tell him. I'm not about to sit back and let this nigga raise my seed so I hope you don't even think that. You got me fucked up if you do."

"Mello it's not as easy as you think it is. Mitch works for my dad. Shit will get sticky, you have to give me time to figure this all out."

I climbed back on top of him and eased down on his manhood. He let out a masculine moan and gripped my hips with his big hands. Mello was a thick man, all muscle but thick. Tall and sexy with his high yellow skin and freckles tracing the bottom of his eyes. If things weren't different I would definitely think about being with him.

Rolling my hips in a circular motion I grinded into him making him forget the conversation we were just having, at least that was my plan. I didn't want to talk about Mitch. I didn't want to talk about this baby, the only thing I wanted to talk about was the way he was making me feel right now.

"Fuck I love you Wynn."

"Ummm baby I love you too." I moaned and threw my head back. Those words weren't all the way false. I did love him and if it weren't for me being with Mitch and everything that he did for me Mello would definitely be a contender.

"Well leave with me. You don't have to stay here and take his shit." He said just as forcefully as he pounded into me from the bottom.

"Take what shit?" that voice sent chills down my spine, it was like malice dripped from every word. Mello threw me off of him and shielded my body with his own.

One thing I knew, even after catching me in a position such as the one that I was in, Mitch wouldn't kill me, he knew that if he did he may as well sign his own death certificate. My father would have his henchmen after him within seconds of finding out what he had done.

"Put the gun down man, it's not what you think."

An evil laugh filled the room and Mitch waved the gun in the air and then fired a shot in Mello's direction. "Move a-fucking-gain and I swear it will be the last time that you do." He hissed.

"Come on man we better than this." Mello was trying his best to reason with him but the shit wasn't working. Mitch was pissed and I could tell by the way he was gripping the gun. "It don't have to be like this."

"You didn't have to fuck my wife either but you did." His voice was calm but his demeanor was anything but. I could feel the hate radiating from his skin.

"Baby listen, I was just mad when I found out about you fucking around with that girl Mira and the Lala chick. I was just mad and I wanted to get you back. That's all it was. Just put the gun down and we can talk about this. You know I love you Mitch." I batted my eyelashes and moved from underneath Mello's hold.

He gave me a look but right now that wasn't important I was trying to save his life and he was just gone have to roll with it. I crawled to where Mitch was standing at the edge of the bed, I lifted up to touch him but he slapped my hands down and shot me in the shoulder.

"Ahhhhhh I cried out in pain."

"Oh, shit baby you okay?" Mello said and Mitch fired another shot his way. "What the fuck you doing man she pregnant."

"You think I give a fuck about that baby? The bastard ain't mine."

"It is yours." I struggled to get out.

"Bitch I had a vasectomy when I married yo hoe ass. I knew I didn't want kids by you. So, I'm shooting blanks bitch." He laughed again.

My confidence in how this was going to play out was slowly fading and I was now looking for a way to get out of this. My phone was on the dresser beside the bed, I was just scared to move. He was unhinged right now and his moves were unpredictable.

"Mitch, I didn't mean for this shit to happen." Mello tried his hands again.

"Yeah me either." He aimed the gun at his head and pulled the trigger.

"Nooooooo! I screamed. When I saw his head hit the pillow and blood splatter everywhere. I knew right then that this would be my last day alive. "Don't do this Mitch, if my dad finds out he's gonna kill you. Just leave."

"Hell, the damage is done right?" he shrugged his shoulders. "I'mma dead man walking, may as well take it all the way."

I went to grab my phone but he fired another shot above my head and I jumped causing the phone to drop on the floor.

"Please Mitch."

"Tell me something, because I've been racking my brain trying to figure out why in the hell you are the way you are. I give you any and everything you need, ya daddy got ya hoe ass spoiled. Why?" He was really searching for answers in my eyes but I didn't have any for him. I was a woman who got what she wanted by any means and I didn't apologize for being me. "Did you love him?"

"No, I love you Mitch."

"No, you just want to survive." He laughed. "You love who's convenient for you and right now I'm it."

"All these years and you can say that shit to me?" I drudged up a few tears and let them fall. He was right, to an extent but I did love him just not as much as I loved myself.

"I actually loved you, yeah I fucked other bitches but I never gave them hoes a second look. You on the other hand was buying whole fucking apartments with my money to fuck other niggas. What kind of nigga you think I am? Nah I can't let that fly."

Things finally caught up to my ass, this was it for me. I went to say something but he lifted the gun and a shot rang out.

CHAPTER 19

Heart

Darren came through with the information that we needed about Mitch. Detective Ringo found the street camera footage that went missing at the time of the shooting. It showed us everything that we needed to know.

I was ready to dead that nigga not only for the shit he been doing around town, or him shooting Lake, but for Lala's pain these last five years. My baby went through all this unnecessary bullshit because his bitch ass didn't feel the need to work his way to the top.

I'm deading his ass on sight. Darren asked us to wait for Wyndel to give the okay but I wasn't a nigga that liked to wait. We were here waiting outside of Darren's house for him to call. If he didn't come through today I was blowing that nigga head off his shoulders by tonight.

"What's up bruh?" I asked Lake when he pulled up beside me. My nigga looked bad like he was carrying around the whole damn universe. "You good my nigga?" I asked him.

He ran his hands down his face and then looked up at me. That nigga was sick as fuck knowing that he lost Mira. That day after we left her house he kept talking about all this shit he was gone do to the nigga Jaxson, I had to tell his ass that it wasn't Jaxson's fault that he fucked up.

The nigga got all pissy and left but I didn't give a fuck I wasn't about to sit there and coddle no grown ass man. He knew what the fuck he was doing when he caused that got damn storm so he needed to man up and handle that shit.

"Mira ain't want nothing to do with ya boy."

"Nigga do you blame her?"

"I fucked up bad Heart."

"Fuck yeah you did and she ain't even trying to hear no apology from yo ass either. My nigga you gotta let her breathe. You can't be over there wilding out and shit because you fucked around on her and she chose not to accept the shit. Let that woman heal. If after she's good she entertains the idea of you again then go for it but if not yo ass just gone have to bite the fucking bullet. But it has to be her choice and you fucking that nigga up ain't gone do nothing but make shit worse."

"If it were you, would you let La move on?" I chuckled at where he was going with this.

"Fuck no I wouldn't! I love that girl too much to see her with anyone else which is why I would never do something so got damn dumb to lose her. I put that shit on my life, I would never put myself in a situation that would cause her to doubt me, to doubt us. Now a nigga ain't perfect but I'll do what I got to do to never hurt her."

"You can say that but you've never been in my shoes."

"Exactly nigga, didn't you just hear what the fuck I just said? I ain't bout to put myself in that situation. Fuck that, on everything I love I'm gone make sure she's nothing but happy."

"Y'all ain't got kids, so it's different." I don't know why this nigga was standing here trying to convince me that his situation couldn't have been avoided when he and I both know that's not the truth.

"Kids made the situation worse fool. They should have been more of a reason for you not to do the dumb shit you did." I slipped my hands in my pockets and shook my head at him.

"Damn nigga!" he dropped his head and shook it. My nigga shit caught up to him and now the only thing left for him to do is to eat that shit like a fucking man.

"Don't be no bitch nigga, whining and over there starting shit with Mira. Let that girl breathe! Yo ass couldn't treat her right so let her find someone who will. Shit!"

"Fuck you Heart." He said and then chuckled, he was clearly frustrated. There was no light at the end of the tunnel for him and it was driving him insane.

"As long as Laken and Larken are good then you should be good. If y'all get to arguing and can't get along the only one that's gone be hurt is them. Show them how much you love them by respecting their mom and her wishes."

"Shut the fuck up with yo Dr. Phil wanna be ass. I'm good nigga, I'm just gone take that shit as a lesson learned. It won't happen again and I put that on my life. I just hope Karma ass have a little mercy on me." We both laughed.

"Nigga she gone have yo ass gone off a stripper that be setting niggas up." I doubled over in laughter and Lake shook his head.

"Don't speak that shit on me nigga."

"Watch and see what the fuck happen."

We chopped it up for a little while before Darren finally pulled up and I mugged his ass. I was pissed the fuck off and ready to handle business so I could fuck my girl silly and live happily ever after without having to worry about shit poppin off.

"Yo what the fuck? You got me sitting here waiting like I'm some kind of bitch. We doing this or not?" The sun was starting to set and I was inches away from stealing off on his ass. If I didn't have the respect that I had for him he wouldn't be standing right now.

"Aye, what's going on?" La and her mom came outside, this was the last thing that I needed right now. I had yet to tell her that Mitch was the one to kill her pops. I wanted that nigga dead and gone before I filled her in on that.

"Hey baby, nothing we bout to go handle some business." I walked up and kissed her.

"Heart you're lying," she searched my eyes, if anyone could read me it was Lala. "What's going on?"

"I gotta tell you something but I need you to chill, I'mma

handle it aight?" she nodded her head but I could tell by her body language that she was lying. "We found out who killed your pops."

"What!" she shrieked. "Who was it? Let's go." She tried to walk past me and get to the car but I snatched her up and brought her to me, I could hear the pain in her voice and that pissed me off even more because she had to go through this shit again. "Let me go." She said with a face full of tears.

"Baby chill let me handle this. I got you and you know it." She fought against my hold. I looked over and saw that Darren had a bawling Cynthia in his arms, I shook my head. This is not what I needed when I was headed out to handle business. My mind was about to be cloudy as fuck.

"Who did it?"

"I'm not about to let you go do nothing dumb. I'll tell you but you got to let me handle this La. I can't be out here doing the shit that I do if I got to worry about you. I need you to chill for me and let me do what I do and that's take care of you." I pulled back so that she could see the seriousness in my eyes. "I'm serious if my head ain't in the game out there because I'm worried about you, that shit could get me killed. I swear to you that Mitch won't be breathing much longer."

"Mitch!" she squealed and I nodded my head. She was pissed off and I knew it but I needed her to understand that if she didn't let me handle this it could be bad for the both of us.

"Laurence baby trust me." She wiped her eyes and then looked at me. For the longest we just stared at each other. We were having a conversation with no words, between the two of us.

"Heart, we gotta go." Darren said with his phone to his ear.

"I love you La aight?" she nodded her head. "Go in the house and lock the doors until we come back. Don't open the door for no one." I pointed at her and she nodded her head again. "Y'all gone need each other today." She looked towards her mother and again she nodded her head.

She crossed her arms across her chest and walked in the direction of Cynt when she got to her they looped their arms and headed in the house to do what we asked. Right before she got in the house she turned to me, "I love you too Heart."

That was all I needed to know, now my head was right and I was ready to go and take care of this nigga. We all piled in the new Tahoe. They impounded my shit when I went after Mitch's bitch ass, hell it was totaled anyway.

"Yo Ringo had someone watching the house and that nigga about to skip town. We gotta move now. I'll take that shit up with Wyndel later."

"Bet." I said as I wove in and out of traffic trying to get to Mitch's house before that nigga got the chance to bail on me. I wanted his life and I wasn't about to let that shit slip through my fingers.

Pulling up we parked a street over and grabbed the heat and headed in the direction of where we knew him to live. When I got to the house I went right to the front door. I knew he had a security system but I didn't give a fuck. I kicked the fucking door in and walked in with my gun pointed and ready to spit.

"What the fuck?" he cried out. *Pop! Pop!* Lake let off two rounds in his right leg before any of us had a chance to do anything. He was pissed. I could tell because he was grilling Mitch while holding his chest.

"Don't cry nigga." Lake taunted. Mitch was sitting there like a bitch, face full of tears. I could see it in his eyes that he was about to start begging but there was no need. Lake cocked his gun back and shot him again this time in his shoulder.

"Ohhhh fuck!" Mitch cried out.

"Put the fucking guns down!" I heard from behind me but I didn't bother moving. Whoever the fuck it was could kiss my ass because the last thing I was doing was putting the fucking gun down. "You can't hear nigga?"

"Fuck you!" I yelled out.

"Aye yo Heart chill." Darren tried to interject but I wasn't paying his ass any attention either. I came here to do something and I wasn't leaving until I fucking did.

"Wyndel, ah shit thank you! Kill this nigga!" he pointed at me and I kicked him in the mouth.

"You kill me bitch!" I growled.

"He killed Wynn." He shouted and I heard someone chamber a bullet. I still didn't move, I guess we were all dying today.

"What do you mean he killed Wynn? I just talk to Wynn." I could hear the humor in his voice. "How can she be dead when she just called me?"

"What? How? That's not possible."

"Why is it not possible? Because you tried to kill her but

didn't make sure that she was dead?" that humor quickly turned evil. "She called me right after she called herself an ambulance. She was passed out after she told me what you did."

"I—I"

"No need to say anything." He said walking over and standing next to me. "Can you put the gun down son?"

"Nah, I ain't ya son. This nigga killed my girl's pops and I promise that he's gone pay for it. I don't give a fuck what you got going on but I'm gone handle this right here, right now."

"So, this must be Heart." He chuckled and so did Darren.

"Yeah that's him." Darren said with a hint of sarcasm in his voice.

"I got something horrible planned for him, I promise that what I can do suits this snake way more than a bullet to the head."

"I feel what you saying but I promised my girl that I would take care of this *personally* and I'mma man of my fucking word!" I cocked my gun and me and Lake let loose into Mitch until neither of us had bullets anymore.

Smoke filled the room and satisfaction filled my soul. Wyndel would just have to deal with the fact that he didn't have a say in how this nigga was gonna die. I was taking his life for La and for Lake. Fuck all that other bullshit.

"He got two bitch ass nephews that are in the county if you want to make an example out of someone but that nigga right there was mine." I shrugged.

"I see you don't like to fucking listen." Wyndel said, his

words were threatening to me anyway. I turned to face him with my empty gun by my side. He chuckled and played with the hair on his chin. "I think you were right D man, they'll do perfect." I glanced out of my eye and Lake was right there with me.

"What the fuck you talking about?" I glanced at Darren and he had a sneaky grin on his face.

"The deal was if yall killed Mitch, I had to find somebody to take over his territory." Darren said looking back and forth between the two of us. "And yall know this shit better than anybody, almost reminds me of me and Big L back in the day." Him and Wyndel laughed, "Almost!" he shrugged and then focused on us to wait for our answer.

I looked at Lake and he looked at me, we both turned to Darren and Wyndel and said, "Bet!" at the same time. We set up a meeting to go over the logistics later. Right now, all I wanted to do was go home and crawl in behind Lala.

When I got back to Darren and Cynt's house, Lake headed home and I went straight in the house. I didn't want to talk to no one, I just wanted to be next to La. I climbed in behind her and she folded her body into mine.

"You know I got you right?" I asked her and she nodded her head, it was dark but I could feel her. "Always and, forever right?" again she nodded. "You know I'll never let anyone hurt you right?" she turned her body around so that she was facing me.

"I know Heart."

"You trust me?"

"Yes!"

"You love me?"

"More than anything."

"Good!" I climbed on top of her and eased into her waiting tunnel and showed her just how much I loved her. This girl was my everything and I couldn't wait to give her the world.

CHAPTER 20

EPILOGUE

M ira
One Year Later

"Oh shit, look at you, on time and shit." I joked as Lake walked up the drive way to pick up the twins.

Things with us were finally in a good place and I was happy about that. He went from barely speaking to me when he came by to get the kids to now we can have full blown conversations about everything that's going on with our lives even the part not involving the kids.

"Nigga shut yo ass up Ms. *I'm running two hours behind because I had to go take my punk ass boyfriend lunch.*" He mugged me and shook his head causing me to laugh.

"Go to hell."

"Only if you meet me there." He pushed past me and headed inside where the kids rushed him. No matter what goes on between me and Lake, the one thing that remains constant was the fact that he was a great father and I loved that about him. "Y'all go get your stuff, so we can go. Uncle Heart and Auntie La are expecting us like now!"

A slither of sadness slipped into my heart at the fact that Lala and I weren't as close as we used to be. When everything happened I kind of shut her out and when things were settling down I was focused on my relationship with Jaxson. We still talked here and there but nothing like we used to.

"Damn I kind of felt like you got the friends in the divorce." I poked my lips out like I was pouting and he flicked my bottom lip.

"That's your fault, you got new friends and forgot about us."

He was referring to the fact that we hang out with Jaxson's friends who I really enjoy being around. They were my age or older and they were all married with kids so they understood my lifestyle more than La did.

Plus, I still wasn't okay with being around the Miracle bitch. In time I would get over it but that shit was a hard pill to swallow for anyone so couldn't anyone expect me to just say forget it and move on. She's reached out to me a few times but I just wasn't ready, when the time comes we'll sit down and chop it up. Nothing will change but I'd give her the conversation.

"Shut up with that."

"Nah for real though we cooking out for La's graduation, you know she got pinned or whatever you call that shit nurses get when they graduate."

"Oh, shit I forgot."

"See, you don't think about the little people anymore." He chuckled right as the twins came tearing down the stairs.

"Whatever Lake, I might just pop up on y'all."

"Come on, I've been meaning to introduce you to Mariela."

"Oh yeah I've heard all about her, that's all Larken talks about. Mariela is a dancer this she taught me that." I rolled my eyes playfully. "Is Miracle gonna be there?" I cringed just saying her name.

"Come on Mira." He threw his head back in frustration. "No, she is more comfortable when I'm not around. We didn't have any ties so when the divorce was finalized she made a conscious decision to steer clear and I'm okay with that."

"Humph well I might just actually stop by then."

"You won't but I'll see you Sunday at 7." He laughed and headed to the door with the kids. "Aye," I called after him and I gave him my attention. "Thank you!" I nodded my head and smiled.

That thank you had more meanings than one and we both knew it. We had a mutual respect and love for each other that no one could take away. We may not be romantically involved but we were connected forever and for the sake of our kids I was completely okay with that.

After I locked up the house I went in the kitchen and started dinner for me and Jaxson. When I say the man was heaven sent he was just that. From his caramel tinted skin to the way his honey colored eyes danced in the sun, everything about this man was amazing and just for me.

In the beginning Lake tried to show his ass, he would pop up without calling and come all times of the night, he tried the *I don't want that nigga around my kids act.* Thank God for sending me a balanced man because even though Lake didn't, Jaxson kept those lines of respect open for the sake of the kids and for me.

He never raised his voice or talked bad about Lake in front of our kids. Even when he wanted to spaz out he held his composure and continued to try and get through to Lake. Finally, when Lake realized that Jaxson wasn't gonna break he stopped with all his bullshit and things became easier for him, us, and the kids.

If you would have told me a year and a half ago that I would be happy with a man that wasn't Lake I would have cursed you out and told you that you were out of your mind. Shit happens and you have to take everything as a lesson learned.

Lake taught me to trust my gut and follow my heart. As bad as I wanted to just take him back and pretend that none of this ever happened I didn't, I knew my worth and I deserved better and I got better.

Jaxson did everything that he said that he would do, he waited around for me to close the door all the way with Lake and for me to heal. He didn't leave me by myself he didn't change up who he was because he felt that I was taking longer than he would have liked.

He was by my side every step of the way and we are celebrating our 6-month anniversary tonight of making it official. It's crazy how life comes full circle. I cheated on Jaxson to be with Lake, who then cheated on me and pushed me back into the arms of Jaxson.

Let Jaxson tell it God was just preparing me to be able to handle a man like him. I guess he was right because before I don't think I would have appreciated the kind of love that he gives. I needed to go through that pain to understand the depths of it.

Knock! Knock! Knock! I don't know why he insists on knocking. I gave him a key a few months ago because he sometimes helps me with the kids when I have to work or if I just need me time.

"Why are you knocking?" I pulled the door open.

"Because this ain't my house." I rolled my eyes. "You can roll em all you want, like I told you until we purchase a house together, I will never feel at home. I'm a man before anything." He leaned down and kissed me before picking me up by my waist. My legs automatically wrapped around his waist and my arms around his neck. He slid his hands down to my ass to hold me up. "Damn did you miss me?"

I tucked my bottom lip between my teeth. "You know I did."

"Well I'm here now. Damn it smells good in here." He started opening up pots with me still in his arms. "You got all this on low?" He asked and I already knew what he was up to.

"Yep."

"Good cause I need you to show me just how much you missed me." He took off up the stairs and laid me down on the bed that he bought when we first got serious. He refused to even lay in a bed that Lake once laid in. "Hey, it's something I've been meaning to tell you."

I looked at him and leaned up on my elbows, I could feel the scowl form on my face and I could tell that he was displeased with it when he stood up and crossed his arms across his chest.

"I'm sorry I just—"

"Just nothing Mira, I'm not him. Stop thinking everything I have to tell you is bad." His face softened a bit and he leaned down and kissed my lips. "I just wanted to say that I was happy that I walked in that bar that day."

"I'm happy you did too." I smiled and leaned up for another kiss.

"I love you Mira, always have always will." It was cliché but my heart skipped a beat and butterflies invaded my stomach. That was the first time he had ever said I love you. Tears flew down my face.

"I love you too Jaxson." He crashed his lips against mine and we spent the next few hours showing each other just how much we loved each other. My heart swelled just knowing that I had a hood love like no other.

CHAPTER 21

*M*iracle

"Girl I'm so proud of you, you have no idea how much." I hugged La around the neck after her pinning ceremony was over.

It was rare for girls like us to make it out of the projects, and we both had found our way out and I was happy for the both of us. There were some bumps. Hell, let me stop lying, there were some big ass mountains in the way but we made our way around them that's all that matters.

Through all of the mess I learned a very valuable lesson, $1+1=2$, it's that simple and if it equals anything else it just doesn't make sense. I made myself believe that what I was going through with a man I thought loved me was normal. I thought that if I accepted his way of thinking that everything would work out in my favor. Boy was I wrong.

One thing I won't do is play the victim because when it all boils down to it I chose to follow that man into the pits of hell and live there. No one made me do that but me and to think I almost lost my life, my friend and my sanity because of it.

Lake moving like he did took a lot out of me and I don't know if I could ever get that back. Our divorce has been final for about four months and I couldn't be happier. Changing my name back to Chaves was the best thing that I could have done for myself.

One good thing came out of the divorce and that was my shop. Lake used it as a guilt gift and I didn't turn it down either. When I saw the building in the divorce settlement I sent him a simple thank you in a text message.

I opened my shop and we've been booming and in business for the last two months. I was proud of me for making it out of the fucked-up situation that I put myself in. I bossed up on myself and handled my business. Now look at me!

I've tried multiple times to apologize to Mira for my part in this whole fiasco but she wasn't having it. I didn't blame her one bit but when the time comes I would be right there with my olive branch.

"Girl I'm proud of us both." She hugged me back.

I was so happy that our friendship was strong enough to withhold the bullshit that it faced. It meant a lot to me that she stood by me through the divorce. To look at us now you would have never known that at one point we almost came to blows on more than one occasion.

"Let me get a picture." Cynt said walking over glowing like

she just stepped out of a magazine. "Look at the two of you, I'm so proud." She beamed and the smile on Lala's face warmed my heart because I remember a time where the only time you would see Cynt sober was when she woke up and that was even rare.

We stood for pictures and then we got ready to pack up, "I really wish you were coming over." Lala whined.

"I'm still not there yet, I would hate to be standing near him and then just get the urge to stab him in the throat." We both laughed.

There was some hurt that still lingered in my heart but it was slowly working its way out. Then and only then would I be able to be in the same room with him and not want to cause him bodily harm.

"I get it but we're on for tomorrow though, right?" she asked.

"Hell yeah, I can't wait. You know how long it's been since I had a spa day?" I looked at her and we both burst out laughing.

"Bitch we've never had a spa day, we from the fucking hood. Shit!" We were laughing so hard that we had grew a little audience that we waved off.

"Shit you know what I mean."

Once it was time to go I said my goodbyes and headed out to my car and to my shop. I had a hair installation to do today anyway. Saturday's were my busiest days but I had to take off for my girl's graduation.

Walking in my shop gave me a sense of peace, something that I vowed to never let another person take ever again. When I get up the courage to date again, I'll make sure that they understand that fully. Until then, I was working on me. I looked down at my watch to check the time and my client for the day was walking in.

"Welcome to Miracle Hair."

CHAPTER 22

*L*ake

Sitting back and watching my kids splash around in the pool had a calming effect on me. Whatever I was feeling or when I got to wanting to do something fucking stupid I looked to them and they made me realize that I had a lot to live for.

After all the shit I put Mira and Miracle through I swore that I would never allow myself to get that wrapped up in bullshit again. All the shit I had going turned my life and my kid's life upside down and I would forever regret my actions.

Me and Mira found a common ground, she gets her child support every month, I paid off the house and got her the Chevy Traverse she been fussing about. At first, I wasn't having that nigga being around my kids and fucking my girl but after a while

I realized that I didn't appreciate what I had, I took for granted that she would always be there.

So, when she left me I didn't know how to handle it, I was wildin. Heart had to talk some sense into my ass again, that and the fact that my kids were suffering because Mira refused to be around my ass and because of that I couldn't see my kids like I wanted to.

Me, Mira and that nigga Jaxson sat down and laid down some ground rules and it turns out he was a pretty cool dude. We ain't cool or no shit like that but I felt like I could trust him around my kids and that helped me sleep better at night.

Once I realized my kids were good I started to work on me and my shit. After we got rid of Mitch's bitch ass we took over Iredell county. Heart locked down Mooresville and the bottom half of Troutman and I got the rest of Troutman and Statesville. That was the biggest move for us in the drug game.

We were pulling in more money than we could even fucking count and that afforded us the ability to take care of our families. Life was good for the most part and I loved that shit.

"What up nigga?" Heart came and joined me at the edge of the pool. I was ready in case something went wrong with the kids. They were strong swimmers but you never could be too sure.

"Not shit just sitting here thinking."

"Don't start that bitch shit again." I flipped his ass off and we both laughed. I will admit for a while I was acting like a bitch but I was good on that shit. I knew what was up. "Where yo girl at?"

he asked and I dropped my head because I knew he was about to say some dumb shit.

"Something came up and she couldn't make it man."

Heart nodded his head with a fucked-up smirk on his face. "Oh, so she ditching yo ass already? I'll just call her Karma."

"Fuck you nigga. I'm good, don't worry about me. Worry about why Lala out here strutting around in that tiny ass bathing suit. Shit sis looking good over there."

"Die nigga." Was all he said before he headed in her direction fussing about her swimsuit. I knew it was only a matter of time until she cursed me out. When a nerf, football came whirling at my head I knew he told her what I said. I looked in her direction and she flipped me off.

Shit may not have been perfect but it was getting there. For once in a long ass time I was happy as hell. I grabbed my Corona and turned it up. Just thinking about how things have changed, a year ago I would be dodging calls from Miracle and Wynn, who no one has seen or heard from, all the while trying to keep Mira happy. The tables have definitely turned, now I'm trying to do right but with the wrong woman.

Looking over at Lala and Heart, I was happy that they found each other I just hoped he didn't fuck it up like me. Sometimes it was hard for me to see Mira happy but I reminded myself that I was the reason that it wasn't me that she was happy with.

I've done some fucked up shit in my life but I promise you it's a lesson learned. Now if I can get my girl on board, I think I'd be okay. I shook my head as Heart's words resonated through my mind, I tried to shake the feeling that he may have been right maybe Mariela was my karma. Only time would tell.

CHAPTER 23

L ala

"Congratulations baby, I'm so proud of you." Heart said as he snuggled up against me in the bed. It had been a long ass day, I had my pinning ceremony and then we had family and friends over for the day. I was exhausted and I knew Heart was too.

"Thank you, baby, for everything that you've done for me. It means the world."

Ever since the night he killed Mitch, things have felt kind of free. It was like a weight was lifted and I had Heart to thank for that. And to think we almost let the woes of the hood keep us from each other. I'm so thankful that we fought through that.

If that bitch Quinia wouldn't have gotten time for the drugs being in the car when her and her sister got caught up with Lil

Jay and Jason then I would have surely had to kill her. I just knew that she wouldn't have let us be.

Word on the street was that after they got popped, somebody gotta hold of lil Jay and Jason on the inside and killed them. When they died, the girls got their charges too and they both were stuck with no bond. That shit sounded fishy to me but I was happy I didn't have to deal with that hoe.

"I'll give you the world if I could." Heart whispered in my ear.

"You're giving me the world baby and you don't even know it." I turned my head so that I could kiss him. "I love you so much."

My words were true, I loved that man more than any words could ever explain. If it weren't for him, me and my mother wouldn't have the relationship that we have now. She was back to the old Cynt, cooking and being a mother. I can't express how much I love it.

Her and Darren are doing great and even though at first it felt weird, I now know that it was God's plan all along. Things have a funny way of working themselves out.

"Love me enough to have my baby?"

"I'll have as many babies as you want as soon as there's a ring on this finger." I held up my left ring finger.

"Remember you said that." He said and then started moving around behind me. He leaned up on his elbow so that he was looking at me. "You are everything that I never thought I wanted. I never knew a love so pure and real until I met you. You gave a nigga a heart and I will forever be grateful. Which is why I want you to be my wife."

He pulled out the most beautiful princess cut diamond from under the pillow. My tears danced in the clarity of the diamond. Was this really happening? I used to dream of this shit from the day I met him on the green box.

Things for us had changed, Heart wasn't just a corner boy selling drugs off the green box. He supplied the boys selling drugs off the green box and even though his line of work is dangerous I believe whole heartedly that he would protect me from it. He had moved us out of the hood and everything already, and I felt safe with him.

I had just graduated from nursing school and I already had a job at a pediatric office. Life was looking up for us and what better way to solidify that than to make it official in the eyes of God?

"There is nothing in this world that I would want more than to be your wife and have all of your bad ass babies." I said through a drenched face.

"You didn't have a choice anyway." He kissed me and then worked his way between my legs.

"What do you think you're doing?"

"Consummating our engagement.

"I don't think it works like that Heart."

"You shitting me." He said as he slid into me and touched my soul with one stroke. This past year or so had showed me a lot about myself and the people around me. I've grown from the feisty little smart mouth girl who didn't have anybody, I was now a woman and about to be someone's wife and mother one day.

Life hasn't been easy for me but it was all worth it. Every single tear brought me to where I was right here, right now and I accept it whole heartedly.

I got my degree, my mom, my friends and A HOOD LOVE LIKE NO OTHER!

 *HE END!*

ALSO BY NIKKI BROWN

Messiah and Reign 1-3

I Won't Play A Fool For You (Messiah and Reign spinoff)

My Love And His Loyalty 1-3

I Deserve your love 1-3

Bury My Heart 1-2

Beautiful Mistake 1-3

Beautiful Revenge

Riding Hard For A Thug 1-3

You're The Cure To The Pain He Caused

Key To The Heart Of A Boss 1-3

I Got Love For A Carolina Hustla 1-3

A Hood Love Like No Other 1-2

CPSIA information can be obtained
at www.ICGtesting.com
Printed in the USA
LVHW041628291018
595208LV00003B/532/P

9 781387 988310